"Litherland's authentic characters and careful research succeed brilliantly in taking me into a delightful vicarious adventure to the Emerald Isle past and present. This insightful journey into the Irish psyche is wise and wondrous and witty."

—Arthur L. Zapel
Executive Editor/Publisher
Meriwether Publishing, Ltd.

CHAIN OF DECEPTION

JANET LITHERLAND

PublishAmerica
Baltimore

First printing

Look to the rainbow. Follow it over the hill and the stream.
Look, look, look to the rainbow. Follow the fellow who follows a dream.

ISBN: 1-4137-5600-X
PUBLISHED BY PUBLISHAMERICA, LLLP
www.publishamerica.com
Baltimore

Printed in the United States of America

This one's for Erma and Diana, the sisters who keep me sane.

Reilly Castle

PROLOGUE

COUNTY KERRY, IRELAND: DECEMBER 1969

Reilly Castle, though nearly four hundred years old, was quite small as castles go. More of a large country home, really. Only two, short crenellated towers stretched toward the Irish sky, one on either side of the massive, brass-studded wood door. But to the tiny child whose wide-eyed gaze pulled her chin higher and higher, the castle was very large indeed.

"Ooo," she cooed softly. "Princess?"

Next to her, the strangers—the kind, portly man and his wife, who had been her companions through many long hours of wet, dreary travel—sighed. The man tugged at his watch fob and checked the time. "No, child. No princess," he replied.

They were early, and he had not yet reached for the heavy doorknocker. He and his wife were bonded couriers, and the child was their "package."

The woman whispered to him, "I don't understand it a'tall. Why did she send only *this* child? Why not the other one, too? And herself! Ulster, especially that godforsaken Derry, is no place for women and children. Shooting, bombing, fires! No place for anyone right now, come to think of it."

The man wiped his brow and straightened his bowler. "Ours is not to question, my dear," he said quietly. He thought about the pretty young woman who had released the child to them. Feisty, she was. Such a handful to deal with. *If she'd been anything to me,* he thought, *anything at all, I'd've, by God, brought her here, too, no matter how much she fussed about it!*

The woman, gazing at the imposing structure before her, whispered, "Such a fine house. For sure 'n they must have means! No need to stay up North in all that turmoil and uncertainty."

The man looked to his right at the thick, lush lawn and the woods beyond. Even at this distance, he could see tiny splashes of color, wildflowers poking up among the trees. *Nothing any prettier than the green grass of Eire,* he thought...*when you can find a quiet patch of it.*

He wiped his eyes and looked at the little girl. Awestruck, that's what she was. Not quite two years old, and this was her first taste of space and peace. Such a pity.

"Robin Reilly, me girl," said the man, steeling himself as he reached for the knocker, "it's time to meet your great-uncle."

~~~

Two months later, the other child arrived at Reilly Castle with similar couriers. By then, however, little Robin was no longer there. Patrick and Anna Reilly had come for her. They had whisked her away to America, to a brand new life on a Florida plantation…to follow a dream.

~~~

The other child, left at Reilly Castle, was forgotten.

PART I

MONTICELLO, FLORIDA
OCTOBER
THE PRESENT

Haviland Plantation

CHAPTER 1

Robin Reilly awoke suddenly at the break of dawn, perspiration clinging to her skin, her muscles tense. She sat straight up in bed, her mouth wide open in a terrifying, silent scream.

The horrible, recurring dream had returned…after many absent years:

I am a child, hiding under something outdoors—I don't know what it is or where it is—and someone is with me. A little friend? We are watching a fire that is very close, so close we can feel the heat and hear the crackling flames. There is a lot of noise. People are running. Then there is a loud bang and a bright light! I scream, trying to call out the name of my friend, but I can't remember it. Over and over again I scream…without making a sound.

This hideous dream had intruded on Robin's sleep five times before— twice when she was very young and her father, Patrick, had comforted her; twice when she was struggling with adolescent problems; and the last time, twenty years ago—right after Anna, her mother, had died. *Why now, after twenty years?*

Briefly, but not seriously, she wondered if she were having a "past life" experience. Her co-worker Jack Tanner frequently arrived at the office with dashing stories of his life as a confidante of Ramses II. But Robin, who thought it was great entertainment, didn't believe a word he said.

She shook her head and ran her fingers through her long chestnut hair, as if those simple gestures could clear her mind.

Still restless after a few minutes, she climbed out of bed, brushed her hair into a low ponytail, and dressed quickly in jeans and a tee shirt. This was Saturday. The rising sun promised beautiful weather, and Robin knew exactly how to shake loose the effects of her nightmare. She grabbed her gun and headed for the woods.

~~~

Greg Haviland angrily made his way through the woods toward home in the mid-morning sunlight, his photo series unfinished and his day ruined. Someone had flushed his covey of quail and shot them right out of the sky. And *not* with a camera! As the beautiful creatures fell to earth, Greg had turned his head away in disgust, ignoring the gnats that stuck to his damp skin. He hated the killing. But he accepted it because that's the way it was, the way it would always be. *Tradition*—a word as holy as the word of God, at least in the plantation South.

He stomped into the "Big House" through the kitchen door. In the old-fashioned kitchen—spacious, masculine and welcoming—two Brumby rockers and a hearth rug rested in front of the corner fireplace though there was seldom need for a fire. The mud he'd dabbed on his skin to conceal himself from the birds had dried, and he'd brushed most of it off outside. Still, bits of it clung to his clothes and hair. He sank into one of the chairs, depositing his camera bag and equipment on the rug.

"That you, Mr. Greg?" called the cook from the pantry. "You need a cold drink?"

"Yes, Berry, to both questions." He leaned forward and began untying his boots.

Strawberry Alice Wheeler could move her bulky, black form faster and more gracefully than any woman Greg had ever known, and he had known her all of his life. She was a descendent of plantation slaves and had said over and over, "They's no job I'd rather do than cookin' in the same big kitchen where my great-great granny cooked." She had no idea how old she was, but she knew that her mother, who had craved strawberries during pregnancy, had taken great pride in naming her Strawberry Alice.

She poured a tall glass of iced tea—sweetened just right—and handed it to her favorite young man. "Mr. Greg, ever' day you come in lookin' like you been wallerin' in a pig pen, 'cept we don' have no pigs. Why don' you clean up, and I'll fix you a nice plate o' cold chicken and sliced tomatoes."

"Not now, Berry. I'm too angry to eat." He pulled off his boots and threw them onto the floor, quickly apologizing to Berry for the dried mud that broke away from them.

She leaned over and peered at his handsome, scowling face, then gently brushed dirt from his eyebrow. "Humph. You're tired, too. Didn' you sleep none last night?"

"Not much." He shook his head, thinking about that damned hunter. For more than a hundred years, hunting parties had paid big money to stay at

Haviland Plantation, pursuing quarry by day and enjoying luxurious living by night. Even Vice President Cheney, with his Secret Service entourage, had hunted quail there. It was a profitable hobby for Greg's grandmother, and it kept the place vibrant. Like the old days. Old Mrs. Haviland loved entertaining in grand style.

"Berry, tell me about the hunting party that's here now," Greg said. "Where did they come from?"

"No one's here, Mr. Greg. They's a group due in from Cleveland, Ohio, on Tuesday night."

Greg glanced up sharply. "But there was a woman out there just now. She moved like a tracker. Shot like one, too. Surprised the hell out of me." He took a swallow of his iced tea.

"Was she pretty?"

"I didn't notice."

"Long, brown hair with bits o' fire in it?"

"Yeah, I guess so."

"Eyes the color o' the north pond in spring?" Berry was teasing him.

"Humph. Who is she? Did she pay to shoot my quail?"

Berry's smile broadened. "That be Robin Reilly, and she don' have to pay. She lives here, remember. Upstairs over the garage. And she's pretty all right."

"Reilly? Patrick Reilly's daughter? No, Robin's just a kid. This was a woman."

"Ummm. How long since you been here for more'n a couple o' days at a time, Mr. Greg? Almos' twenty years! Kids grow up. Why, Robin's done been to college, been married and divorced, and has her a fancy job in Tallahassee, somethin' to do with them newfangled 'puters." With knowing pride, she strode to the worktable and began icing her caramel layer cake.

Greg leaned back in his chair. *Little Robin Reilly...a grown woman?*

~~~

Robin arranged the last of the pastry strips on her quail pie, set it in the oven, and closed the door. She hadn't hurried because Patrick, her father, was out shopping for auto parts, something he did carefully and with much pleasure. She walked out onto the second-story screened porch that overlooked the driveway and parking area. Directly beneath her was a bricked and pillared ten-car garage and repair shop, where her father kept the odd assortment of Haviland vehicles in top condition and scrupulously clean—a Rolls Royce, a Lincoln, a Chevy station wagon for the household staff, and a Jaguar XJ6, which Greg drove when he was "in residence." Approached from the back was a drive-in basement for a Range Rover, a pickup truck for Patrick's use, and Robin's Ford compact. Also housed in the basement was Patrick's pride and joy—his 1961 Cadillac, restored. Robin lovingly called it the "Turquoise Batmobile," referring to its odd color and long fins.

Grateful for the pleasant weekends spent with her father in her childhood home, Robin stretched her tired body and inhaled deeply of the fresh evening air. Lights at the Big House began to twinkle in the distance. Since the Jaguar was not in the garage below, she knew Greg had come home again. In a way, she was sorry they had grown up because somehow over the years she had lost touch with a childhood friend.

She kicked off her sandals and sat on the padded porch glider, gently rocking it back and forth. Cicadas were singing, and after a few moments she became so mesmerized by their tuneless music that she was only vaguely aware of the telephone's ringing, floating out from the kitchen. Its insistence finally prodded her tired mind.

"Robin? This be Berry. I was jes checkin' to see if you was there. Uh, Miss Emily and me, we, uh, wants to bring you some homemade ice cream." Her voice sounded strange.

"Now?" Robin asked. She couldn't remember the last time Mrs. Haviland, whom everyone called Miss Emily, had come to visit, though Robin had spent many delightful evenings in the old woman's parlor.

"We be right over." Berry hung up.

What on earth…? Robin slipped her feet back into her sandals, pulled off her apron, then hurriedly straightened the magazines on the coffee table. The "loft," as one of Robin's friends had named the garage apartment, had three bedrooms, two baths, a living room with a fireplace, and a huge kitchen-dining room. The elevator, installed by Mrs. Haviland when Robin's mother, Anna, had become ill, was seldom used after Anna's death. Both Patrick and Robin preferred the stairway.

In a few minutes a car pulled up below, and Robin heard the steady hum of the elevator. She unlocked the front door and waited in the exterior foyer until Miss Emily and Berry emerged. They were not carrying ice cream.

~~~

"Mr. Greg be home. He brought us," Berry explained as she ushered Mrs. Haviland into the living room. "Had to squat to get into that car o' his, it's so low to the ground." She helped settle the older woman onto a straight chair, the only kind she ever sat in. "Mr. Greg's just back from Australia. One o' them 'photo shoots' he calls 'em."

"He's downstairs, dear," Mrs. Haviland injected before Robin could respond. "I asked him to check on the cars."

Emily Haviland, though eighty-six years old, was mentally alert and in remarkable physical condition. She was a thin woman, who always wore dresses trimmed in lace and had her hair "done" once a week in a tight-curl style as old as her age. Now, she sat erectly on the edge of her chair, which was the way she always sat. She considered it "ladylike." Tonight, though, she held herself even straighter, and her eyes were open a bit too wide. Berry stood respectfully by her side.

"May I get you some tea?" Robin asked uncertainly.

"No, thank you, dear." She said nothing more, just sat quietly, twisting a linen handkerchief through her fingers.

Finally, Robin lowered herself onto the sofa, an ominous, leaden feeling taking shape in the pit of her stomach. "What's wrong?" she asked.

Berry moved to Robin's side as Mrs. Haviland said, "You must be strong, dear. We have received word that your father's pickup truck was involved in an accident on Highway 90. He was coming home from Tallahassee."

"How is he?"

The old woman's wide-held eyes could no longer contain the unshed tears, which now spilled softly over her wrinkled skin. She was a sweet and gentle person, who regretted that her next words would be hurtful. "He did not survive."

Berry gathered the stunned Robin into her arms. At first Robin thought there must be a mistake. *This isn't happening.* "Are you sure?" she asked.

"We sure," Berry answered.

Robin was still too shocked to cry. "How did it happen? Where is he?"

Mrs. Haviland dabbed at her tears and answered, "There was a wide load—a 'manufactured home,' I believe they're called now—coming toward Patrick's truck. It hung over his side of the road as he met it at the top of a hill."

"But why didn't he see it? Weren't there any flashing lights? Didn't the thing have an escort car in front of it?" Robin's voice rose with each question as she, too, rose from the sofa.

"We don't know the details yet, dear. Berry, go fix her something to drink."

"No! No, thank you. I'm all right. I...I just need some time to take it all in." Robin's hands began to tremble, then to shake.

"I called Graydon Funeral Home to take care of immediate needs. If you want to do differently, arrangements can be made in the morning." Mrs. Haviland stood. "Right now you need to rest. Berry's going to spend the night with you, dear, and she has a sleeping pill I want you to take."

"That's not necessary. It really isn't. I'll be fine by myself." Robin's voice cracked as she spoke. She wasn't fine at all.

Just then the elevator hummed again and Berry said, "That be Mr. Greg comin' for his gran'mama. I'll just see her to the elevator and be right back."

Miss Emily moved to kiss Robin on the forehead. "You're made of fine Irish stock, Robin, my dear. You'll cope. Let Berry know if there's anything you need. Anything at all."

They went out the door, and Berry was back in less than a minute.

Robin still had not cried. Automatically, she went to check on the quail pie, Patrick's favorite dish. He never made it for himself. Always loved the way Robin made it. The crust was just beginning to brown. It smelled so good. *Surely this is all a mistake*, she thought. *Surely Patrick will come up the stairs any minute now, whistling one of his Irish ditties. He'll spend the evening carving wood or cleaning his guns.* He had taught Robin to love and respect guns; he had taught her to shoot and to hunt. No one could've been prouder of her than Patrick. *Dear Patrick.* She'd always called him Patrick. Everyone on the plantation did.

"Robin, honey, take this pill, then let me tuck you in like you was a chile." Berry had come up behind her with a glass of water. "And don' you worry none 'bout the pie. I'll take it out when it's jes right."

Robin swallowed the pill and mechanically got ready for bed.

"I'll be right there in the next bedroom tonight," Berry said as she tucked the covers under Robin's chin. "You know I loves you like you was my own."

~~~

16

Alone in the dark, Robin thought of Patrick hunting quail; she thought about their rides in the Turquoise Batmobile, their picnics near the plantation's lake, their long talks about college and about "following the dream," whatever the dream might be. Patrick had followed his dream. He had left his home in Ireland and come to America to make a new life for himself, for his wife, Anna, and for Robin. But Anna's dream—to someday have a little shop to sell the Irish lace she made so beautifully by hand—had died with her. And Patrick...Patrick...

Finally, slowly, Robin wept.

CHAPTER 2

Greg ushered his grandmother into the private sitting room adjoining her bedroom. "I'll send Ardith up to help you get ready for bed," he offered.

"No, not just yet," she said. "Stay with me for a little while." She sat, or rather "perched," on the edge of the old Duncan Phyfe sofa and motioned for him to join her. The low table in front of them held a bowl of freshly cut roses and several copies of large-print *Reader's Digest* magazines. Other tables were laden with knick-knacks and framed snapshots. The room was cluttered and cozy.

Greg pulled a lumpy afghan from behind him and tossed it onto a wing chair. "What can I do to help you, Gran?" he asked.

"Go see Robin in the morning. Ask about her preferences for funeral arrangements; she'll certainly want her friends and co-workers notified. You might call Mr. Whitaker and Mr. Colson up in New York. Patrick was their special hunting guide every year for at least ten years." She sighed, tears returning to her eyes. "Oh, Greg, Patrick was here for so many years. More than thirty. I'm going to miss him very much, especially his cheerful demeanor."

"I'll miss him, too, Gran. Did he have relatives in Ireland? Robin's grandparents, uncles, aunts?"

Mrs. Haviland considered but shook her head. "I'm quite sure that when Anna passed away, Patrick told me they had no family. At least none came for Anna's funeral." She dabbed at her eyes.

"Shall I call the Davis' cottage to see if they're home yet?"

"Please, dear. Cassie's going to be very upset when she hears about Patrick. She and Robin have been close friends since they were children. Oh, and ask her if she'd please relieve her mother at Robin's home in the morning. Goodness knows Berry's going to have her hands full, what with the funeral and that hunting party arriving on Tuesday. They'll expect the usual." The "usual" meant a magnificent dinner at the long table in the main dining room, followed by fruit liqueur served in one of the mansion's four drawing rooms.

Greg used the phone on the table beside him, but there was no answer. Cassie and Jerome were still out for dinner and a movie. He glanced at his grandmother and caught her stifling an unladylike yawn.

"It's time you were in bed, Gran," he said, standing. "I'll send Ardith up now."

"Do keep trying to reach Cassie, dear."

He bent his head and kissed her cheek. "Don't worry. I'll take care of things."

~~~

When Greg tapped on Robin's door the next morning, he was greeted by Cassie Davis and the smell of fresh-brewed coffee.

"Robin's awake, and I've insisted that she eat," Cassie said. "Omelets and fruit. Would you like to join us?"

Greg nodded and followed her into the kitchen.

"Thanks for calling last night," Cassie said. "Jerome and I were devastated by the news, but I just had to be here when Robin woke up. She's been like a sister to me." She began cracking eggs into a bowl. "Mama left about an hour ago."

"Are you sure this isn't too much of a strain on you?" Greg asked.

"You mean because of my pregnancy?" She smiled, gently patting her tummy. "Not at all. I may be seven months along, but I'm healthy as a horse." Cassie was an LPN at the county medical center and had just begun a three-month maternity leave. "Have a seat, Greg. Or should I call you *Mr. Greg,* now that we're grown up?"

Greg rolled his eyes. "No, thanks," he said, wryly. "When someone calls me 'Mr. Greg,' it makes me feel, well…old." He grinned. "Is thirty-six old these days?"

Cassie laughed. "I certainly hope not." She was glad to see he hadn't changed. It was almost like they were kids again. She laid plates, napkins and silverware on the round oak table, and Greg set the places.

Robin came into the kitchen-dining area just as he was folding the napkins. She looked from the domestic-acting Greg to her best friend, feeling an overwhelming sense of gratitude, and fresh tears sprang to her eyes. Greg quickly helped her into a chair, then sat across from her as Cassie put the food on the table.

Robin blinked away her tears and hugged her robe closer to her body—the white robe with a fuzzy green shamrock on the pocket, the one Patrick had given her last Christmas. She looked up at Greg and with the tiniest of smiles said, "Don't I know you from somewhere?"

Greg chuckled. "It's been that long, has it?"

Robin nodded. "The last time we had a conversation of any substance was when Cassie and I were eleven and you were twelve."

Greg looked puzzled.

"You don't remember? Ironically, it was a funeral. My dog, Snap, had been mistaken for a rabbit by one of the hunters, and you brought him home to me. Do you remember, Cassie?"

"Sure I do." She pulled up a chair and joined them at the table. "Patrick was away from the plantation, so Greg dug a grave behind the garage."

"Oh, yes," he said. "I recited part of the Twenty-Third Psalm, as much as I could recall, and Cassie sang a verse of something."

"'Beyond the Sunset,'" Cassie said. "Then the three of us sat by the grave and waited for Patrick."

Robin put down her fork, the omelet untouched. "Patrick won't come this time."

"Robin," Greg said. "Try to eat something. I want to talk with you about some practical matters." He took paper and pen from his pocket. "Family and friends will have to be notified, and I'd like to do it for you. Can you help me make a list?"

Robin sighed and picked up the fork once again. "Let's see, there's Mr. Durbin, my boss. He can tell my friends at work. And I suppose someone ought to call Tripp Nicholson, my ex-husband. He liked Patrick very much." She thought a moment. "I guess that's all. My work and the plantation, that's all I've had time for. Don't know anyone else." She stabbed a slice of fresh pineapple with her fork.

"What about John and Barbara Marchant at the gun club?" Cassie asked.

Robin nodded and bit into the pineapple slice.

"I'll get the addresses for you, Greg," Cassie offered.

"Is there any family, Robin?" Greg asked.

"You're looking at it. Cassie, Jerome, Berry, your grandmother and you. The plantation is my home; the plantation people are my family."

"Is there anyone, uh…anyone in Ireland who needs to be notified?"

Robin shook her head. "Patrick said when he and my mother decided to emigrate, there was nothing left for them in Ireland. They had sold everything they owned, added that money to their savings, and moved to America to start a new life for the three of us. My mother said she'd had enough of bombs and fighting. Her parents both died in the 'troubles.' *Troubles*. What an inane term for such horror." She blinked back new tears. "America—that was Patrick's big dream. He was afraid I'd end up a spinster in Ireland since I had no dowry, and he believed I would have more opportunity here."

"You've certainly done all right," Cassie said, patting Robin's arm, "and Patrick was so proud of you. He told me he had no idea what a computer systems analyst was, but his Robin was the 'best damned one of those things' on the job!"

Robin couldn't help smiling.

Greg tried one last time. "Did he ever say anything about his parents or aunts and uncles?"

"His parents, like my mother's, died somewhere in Northern Ireland before I was born. Patrick was a great talker—he had the Irish 'gift of the gab,' and loved to talk about Ireland—but he never wanted to talk much about family, and I didn't press him. As for aunts, uncles, cousins—he said all that were left were 'shirt-tail' relations. Sometimes he slipped and called them 'shit-tails,'" she added wryly. "Odds and ends who wouldn't know Patrick Reilly's family from Noah's two giraffes. That's a direct quote."

Greg put away his paper and pen. "I'll contact these people today," he said.

"There's one thing, though…" Robin started, then paused. "Oh, I wish I'd asked him more questions."

"About what?"

"Well, during the past two weekends, when I came to visit him, he talked about making a trip to Ireland. It was strange because he'd never had any desire to return. Then all of a sudden it became almost an obsession, as if he *yearned* to see the land of his birth one more time during his life. He had flight schedules, maps. And he asked Miss Emily for some time off."

"When did he intend to go?"

She shrugged. "I don't know. He said he wasn't sure. But it must have been soon, the way he was planning. He even bought a new suit—" Her voice broke, and she stood. "I guess there'll be another use for it now. Please excuse me. And…thanks for coming, both of you," she added, quickly leaving the kitchen.

The room was very quiet for a few moments.

"Well, what do you think, Cassie?"

"What do I think?"

"Will she be all right?"

"Sure. But she'll need some time. She and Patrick were very close."

Greg pushed his chair back and rose slowly. "So close he wouldn't talk to her about her family? So close he didn't plan to take her to Ireland with him?" He started for the door.

"Don't be too hard on Patrick, Greg. He was a little quirky, but he was a good person. And he did love Robin. No doubt about that."

Greg let himself out and walked to the Big House in the morning sun. Something bothered him. Something Robin had said....

~~~

There was quite a gathering at Monticello's Oakfield Cemetery on Tuesday morning. Gelling's Flower Shop had arranged a beautiful spray of roses for the top of the casket—Robin had trusted them to do it just right. There were arrangements of carnations and orchids from Haviland Plantation and white lilies from the company where Robin worked. All of the colorful flowers were made even more beautiful by the misting October rain.

Plantation folk and friends stood without umbrellas as Father Howard delivered an appropriate message. Robin liked the priest. He always wore a brown alb tied at the waist with a rope, looking very much like an ancient monk. Patrick had been passionately religious. "Always stay close to your Catholic upbringing, darlin'," he had said. "If things in your life ever get all mixed up, you'll be glad you did. Remember this. It's fine advice." Robin cherished the memory.

Mr. Durbin, Robin's boss, was there; so were the Marchants and so—to Robin's surprise—were the Whitakers and Colsons from New York, who had flown in just for the funeral, which was graveside only. Whitaker and Colson had been two of Patrick's favorite hunters—wealthy "Yankees," each with his own private airplane.

Jack Tanner from Robin's office was there, too, assuring her that Patrick would be reincarnated; and, of course, Tripp Nicholson, Robin's ex, who had her arm tightly linked in his. Many of the plantation workers were there, looking very sad indeed. Robin had seen Greg with his grandmother, but Cassie and Berry were back at the plantation, cooking the food that would be served buffet style to everyone who went to the Big House following the funeral. After-funeral gatherings sometimes seemed a bit irreverent, even party-like, but they did relieve tension and provide a catharsis of sorts.

Father Howard was saying, "An old Irish proverb tells us that one is truly happy only if one can die happy. I believe we can safely say that Patrick ·Brannigan Reilly was a truly happy man."

The mist was getting heavier. Strangely, through the mist and over the drone of Father Howard's voice, Robin heard whistling. A cheerful Irish ditty. She perked up her ears, then smiled to herself, realizing the sound was coming from her own heart. Patrick would always be with her. She looked up at Tripp, reassured by his familiar blond good looks and warm smile. They didn't love each other anymore, possibly never did, but they were friends, and she did feel comfortable with him.

Greg Haviland pushed his damp hair out of his face, wishing Father Howard would wind things up. He looked at Robin through the crowd of people and wondered how she could be so content with an ex-husband.

~~~

That night Robin was exhausted, physically and emotionally. She had told Cassie that she wanted to be alone and had kindly, but firmly, declined Tripp's offer to stay with her. She dressed for bed early and tried to read, hoping to take her mind off the last few days. The extra sleeping pill Cassie had left still lay on the bedside table. Rain was falling full force now, and after just ten minutes of listening to its rhythmic pelting, Robin turned out her light...but couldn't go to sleep.

She thought about Patrick; about her mother, Anna; her own failed marriage; even her long-dead dog, Snap. And she felt a sudden sense of terrible loss and loneliness. She wished, now, that she had pressed Patrick for more information about the early years. Even if her relatives in Ireland really were "shit-tails," she wished she knew who they were. For the first time in her thirty-five years, she wondered who *she* was.

CHAPTER 3

Mr. Durbin had graciously given Robin the rest of the week off, and she had accepted with relief, welcoming the time to put things in order, which was the way she lived her life. Orderly. No loose ends. Now she had to deal with Patrick's affairs, including his planned trip to Ireland. She needed to know what that was all about. She'd have to clean out his things and pack her own, for the garage apartment would certainly be needed for Patrick's replacement and family.

She stood in the doorway of her bedroom, remembering fondly her growing-up years. Anna had been a "stay-at-home mom" long before that phrase was coined. She was talented in all things domestic, yet always had time to play with Robin, help with homework, and listen to her daughter's adolescent woes. Robin could talk with Anna about anything. Anything at all. *If she were just here now,* Robin thought.

She looked around her bedroom, which hadn't changed much since she left it for a college dorm and later an apartment of her own. The draperies, which Anna had made of ivory corduroy to keep out the hot southern sun, still hung at the windows; and the matching bedspread was neatly in place, as it never was during Robin's teen years.

She remembered transferring from the public school to a nearby private school in the ninth grade—not because she wanted to but because Miss Emily had convinced her parents that it was absolutely necessary if Robin were to become a "well-rounded young woman." Robin smiled at the thought. She was sure the ploy had not been successful. The private school with its stern headmaster and demanding instructors was certainly inhibiting.

Yes, her bedroom had been her childhood refuge—a place she could snuggle away from the world, whether that meant playmates or school or insistent boyfriends. As a "late-blooming" teenager (another of Miss Emily's expressions), she wasn't ready for the groping other girls enjoyed in the back seat of a car. It was only during her college years that she cast her inhibitions aside and became, uh…well rounded.

Then she thought of her recurrent nightmare and the times she'd pulled the covers over her head, trying to shut it away. That certainly was a "loose end" she'd like to tie up!

She moved to her closet and pulled out the traditional white jacket she wore when occasionally serving as a hunting guide. She then picked up her Browning over-and-under, 20-gauge shotgun and headed for the outdoors. She wasn't planning to hunt, but she wore the jacket to identify herself to possible poachers. She took the gun simply because she liked the feel of it in her hands. It was her favorite. Patrick had given it to her as a reward for downing her first quail.

Bits of morning sunlight peeped through the cloud cover, but the air was cool and moist after rain. If the weather held, it would be perfect for quail hunting. She was glad that Haviland's hunting season was ten weeks longer than the regular season. It gave her an early start and some of the best weather. Right now, though, she just wanted to get away from her own troubling thoughts.

She chose a pinestraw path leading to the woods. There were paths to the lake, some to the camellia gardens, and some that were marked to provide guests with a safe, walking tour of the upper part of the plantation. Her path widened at the edge of the piney woods, then gradually faded into groundcover.

Robin continued walking for about a mile. Each step seemed to give her more energy, more strength, and when she finally sat on a fallen log to rest, she had discovered a measure of peace within herself. She was proud of being Irish and Catholic and part of the American dream, Patrick's dream. Patrick had given her that and a whole lot more. Even her love of hunting was part of her carefully nurtured heritage. "You remind me of me dear mother, God rest her soul," Patrick had said, the familiar twinkle in his eye, "a gun in your arm, stalking the birds. That's the way the Irish raise their women, you know."

"And how is that?"

Robin blinked and turned to her right, seeing nothing, realizing that she had spoken her last sentence aloud.

The voice asked again, "How do the Irish raise their women?" She knew it was Greg, but she still could not see him.

"With a gun in the arm, a red setter at the heels, and a love of stalking pheasants," she called out.

"Is that what you're hunting?" he asked. He stepped into view, brushing pinestraw from his hair.

"This isn't pheasant country, and I'm not hunting today."

"Then why the gun?"

"I like the feel of it. What are you hunting?" she asked, indicating the camera hanging from his neck.

"I always have a camera," he said, "just in case. I like the feel of it."

Robin's sudden smile softened her features. "I have an idea," she said. "Why don't Max and I take you quail hunting. We'll find the birds and flush them, and you take all the photos you want."

"Who's Max?"

"The pointer. My dog."

He grinned. "That's a great idea. When?"

"Today. Mid-afternoon. The conditions should be perfect then, and there won't be any hunters working the property until tomorrow. We'll have it all to ourselves."

He pulled at his chin. "No hunters to shoot my quail out from under me?"

She shook her head. "None."

"Like happened on Friday."

"What? Who shot your quail?"

"You did."

Robin was speechless.

"I found the covey," he said, "and, in fact, had taken several long shots through the brush. Then, suddenly, you appeared out of nowhere, flushed them, and uh, well.... "

"Oh, Greg, I'm sorry. I didn't know."

"Made me mad as hell," he said, grinning. "And I didn't dare show myself. I'd been there a long time and had covered most of my body with mud."

She laughed. "I owe you a good hunt this afternoon, and you won't need mud. Three-thirty at the kennels?"

"Great. I'll be there."

Robin watched him as he walked back toward the Big House. In a way, he reminded her of Patrick—physically, that is. He was taller than Patrick, and his hair was a bit darker, but they both had strong facial features and eyes that absolutely glistened. She couldn't help smiling as she turned and went farther into the woods.

~~~

Emily Haviland was enjoying her late-morning coffee on the back terrace. From her comfortable old wicker chair she could look down the wide expanse of lawn to the quiet little lake where ducks paddled along, unconcerned with "people problems." She could see the gazebo at the end of the dock, a whim that her late husband had provided for her. When she sat in the gazebo, it seemed as if she were alone on the lake, the only person in her immediate world. It was a wonderful place for reading novels. Murder mysteries. Especially those of Agatha Christie. Lately, though, she did her reading on the terrace or in her sitting room because the walk to the gazebo was simply too tiring. Yes, Mrs. Haviland may have been eighty-six, but in her heart she felt more like fifty. *Why does the body play such awful tricks on one?* she wondered. She had battled stiffness for several years, and lately she'd noticed a slight hunch in her shoulders that wouldn't go away no matter how she pushed and straightened herself.

It was nice to have Greg home for a while. She wasn't sure if he'd come home to photograph quail or if he were photographing quail as an excuse to come home. She smiled, suspecting the latter. He'd always loved the plantation, though she was glad she'd insisted on the Virginia boarding school for him. Otherwise, he would have been with his parents in that terrible crash of their chartered plane. *Always traveling,* she thought with dismay, as she remembered her son and his lovely wife.

She took a deep breath and let it out slowly. Greg was her sole heir now. *Heir to a hunting plantation, and he despises hunting.* She chuckled softly.

"Gran?" Greg was coming up the steps at the side of the terrace. "What's so funny?"

"You are, dear boy," she answered with another chuckle.

"What did I do?" He pulled up a chair and sat beside her.

"I was just thinking about you, about the paradox of your owning this place one day, and about the utter confusion when you try to run it."

"Oh, I'll still entertain hunters here."

"You will?"

"Yes. But they'll hunt with cameras instead of guns. I might even sponsor photography classes that could be set up in the old school rooms."

"Why, Greg, what a marvelous idea! Maybe we should start making plans now because when I die—"

"Which won't happen for many more years," Greg injected. "In the meantime, this is your house and your land, and you must run it in the way that pleases you most." Greg knew that this well-run business of his grandmother's was what kept her healthy and younger than her age. He dearly loved her.

Her eyes twinkled. "Then we'll continue to shoot here at Haviland, and when it's your turn and you transform the gun rooms into darkrooms, I want you to know that I'll applaud you from my grave for doing what you believe in."

"You really don't mind?"

"Of course not. Shall we have a glass of tea before lunch? You *are* having lunch with me, dear?" It was more statement than question.

~~~

They had their meal at the square mahogany table in the family dining room, much smaller though no less elegant than the room where twenty could be easily seated and served. Gilt-framed paintings of days gone by adorned the walls, and a fine collection of Hummel figurines glistened behind the glass of a locked and lighted curio cabinet.

Berry had prepared homemade rolls, a squash casserole, and tomatoes stuffed with chicken salad. Greg wasn't overly fond of squash, but he made an effort to eat a small portion. Miss Emily still encouraged her grandson to eat everything on his plate; as for herself, she always left a tiny bit of everything. Why? "To show that I'm dainty and don't require a lot of food," she'd answered when Greg had asked long ago. It was a good thing the twelve-year-old had kept his comment to himself. *Bullshit,* he'd thought as he'd grinned at his beloved Gran.

When they had finished and Greg had gone, Mrs. Haviland made her way to the kitchen to discuss the next day's meals with Berry. There would be just six in the party: four seasoned hunters and two novices.

"Deer sausage, eggs, grits, and homemade biscuits for breakfast, Berry," she said. "Keep in mind that all of our hunters this time are men, and they did not bring their wives along. No fussy little breakfast casseroles, please."

"Yes, ma'am. Might they like quail for dinner?"

"Certainly, Berry," she replied. "I think the quail with green grapes and hazelnuts that you do so well. And some wild rice."

"What about the wine, Miss Emily?" Berry asked.

"The wine...something different, I think. Let's get a *Clos Vougeot* from the cellar." She thought a moment. "Yes, that will be different. And, Berry, there will be *nine* for dinner tomorrow evening."

"Nine, Miss Emily?"

"The six hunters, myself, Greg...and Robin Reilly." She touched her index finger to her cheek as a tiny smile sprung from somewhere deep inside her, growing bigger and bigger and bigger.

CHAPTER 4

"Over here," Greg called to Robin. He had arrived at the kennels first and was leaning on the fence watching the dogs play. When his grandfather was alive and the plantation was operating at its peak, the kennels had sheltered nearly seventy hunting dogs—foxhounds, pointers, and setters. Now there were only a dozen or so. "Which one's Max?" he asked.

"The one staring at you with uncertainty in his eyes," Robin replied.

Roy Blanton, the trainer, delivered Max to Robin with a cheery "Good hunting!" and they were off toward the woods on foot.

"Does Max know I'm not a real hunter?" asked Greg.

"Sure he does. You're not carrying a gun, and it's a safe bet that your hunting britches don't have that seasoned smell he's used to."

"Thank God! Is that why you brought your gun? For Max?"

"For me. I have an aversion to rattlesnakes. I decided we'd walk rather than take the horses," she continued. "There will be quail on the south end, not too far from here, and we'll have more freedom that way. Max is a close-working dog, so we don't have to worry about losing him."

As they got closer to their destination, the umbrella of pine trees shaded the ground, allowing only small splashes of sunlight to brighten the woods. Tall clumps of gallberry were all around, shielding the hidden coveys of quail. Max zigzagged out in front, his nose close to the ground. If he got too far away, Robin's "Back, Max!" would bring him to her immediately.

Suddenly, Max froze in the classic point, head and tail stretched high. Robin had briefed Greg—exactly what to expect and what to do. Excitement surged through his body like electricity! As Max held the point, Robin and Greg moved forward. At her signal Greg stopped, and she moved in, flushing the covey. Greg's camera was up and ready as nearly twenty birds sprung from the ground, their wings making a symphonic whirring sound. It was a perfect shoot!

"If you want to get the next group up faster," Robin said, "we'll let Max flush them. They respond much differently to a dog."

31

During the next few hours Greg was able to photograph four different coveys. Earlier in the afternoon he had asked Robin, "How do you know for sure what a quail is going to do?"

She gave him the same answer Patrick had given her when she was a child: *You know for sure what a quail is going to do only after he does it.* "You think, you plan, then you go with your best guess," she added.

~~~

Robin stretched out in bed that night, thinking it had been just about the best day she'd ever had in the woods. And right on top of that thought came feelings of guilt because it was only one day after Patrick's funeral. How could she even think of having a good time so soon? Just when she was sure she had everything together, she didn't. When she felt in control, she wasn't. She wondered if her confusion was normal. Was it part of grieving? That night she took another of Berry's sleeping pills, unaware that her grief had just begun.

~~~

Dinner started pleasantly enough. The six hunters, plus Greg, Robin, and Mrs. Haviland, were in the formal dining room, where a collection of Audubon prints hung pretentiously around the walls. A huge oriental rug covered the floor, leaving plenty of space around the edges for the lovely hardwood to show, and in the middle of the rug sat the cherry dining table, adjusted shorter to accommodate nine chairs. The occasion called for candlelight and crystal. One of the eleven sets of fine china from the "dish pantry" sparkled on the gold damask cloth.

Robin had sometimes been invited to these "socials," which seemed to give Miss Emily so much pleasure, so she knew what to expect and how to dress. She had chosen a deep blue silk dress trimmed with silver thread. Her shimmering dark hair was pinned loosely behind her ears to show off the only pair of diamond earrings she owned, a twenty-first-birthday gift from Patrick, who'd probably saved his money for a long, long time to buy them. She looked terrific and she knew it. Miss Emily fussed over her, as she always did, but the men absolutely *ogled.* And the look on Greg's face when he first saw her could only be described as astonishment. All during dinner she felt his gaze on her, and it was much different from the way he had regarded her in hunting gear! Why, then, did the evening have to end so *badly?*

32

Mrs. Haviland always guided the conversation during meals to "acceptable" topics, ruling out any that might give offense, which left little more than family life and the weather. During dessert, however, she would sit back and "go with the flow" (her personal cliché), which in a roomful of hunters meant the hunt. Mrs. Haviland enjoyed this every bit as much as the hunters did. But as the conversation progressed on this particular evening, Greg became noticeably withdrawn, and to Robin, he looked increasingly hostile. This would have been the right time for him to excuse himself or for his grandmother to bring up the weather, but the older woman was unaware.

"The flush is an almost indescribable thrill," one of the new hunters was saying. "The first time, I wasn't ready for that… that *burst* of brown bodies exploding into space! All I could do was watch. By the time I shot, they were out of range."

"I'm sure you did fine the next time," Robin offered, knowing full well that her place was to encourage the guest and to make him feel good about himself.

"Yeah, I chose a bird, swung my gun, pulled the trigger, and he folded like a dishrag!"

Greg put his coffee cup down with such force it startled everyone. Robin felt heat rising to her face.

"He did better than I," said the other rookie, pretending not to notice. "With the first two coveys, I shot nothing but treetops."

"You just need confidence," said one of the veterans. "The more confidence you have, the more you kill. Tomorrow you'll do great."

Greg rose. "Grandmother, Robin, gentlemen, please excuse me. I am not comfortable discussing the killing of wildlife."

"Ah, come on, man. It's a sport," said one of the men.

Robin, tense as a porcupine posed to attack, crossed her fingers and prayed that Greg would not say "blood sport."

Mrs. Haviland intervened, clearly upset, but it was much too late to discuss the weather. "Hunting is most practical," she offered weakly.

"With due respect, Gran, I've heard that argument before."

"It's a good argument, Greg," Robin said. "Designated hunting seasons prevent year-round depletion of wildlife. They also thin out overpopulation, so life will be better for animals and humans alike."

Greg glared at her, which only served to instill more fire in her justification.

"On this acreage alone we have deer, bobcat, gray fox, squirrel, rabbit, turkey, and droves of flying ducks!" she said. "If game were not thinned, you wouldn't be able to walk across this property, never mind take pictures! It *is* a practical sport, Greg. It makes sense," she added, slightly more subdued.

"Yes, it makes sense," said Greg, still glaring at her. "You give every helpless bird a sporting chance to live or die." With that, he left the room.

~~~~

Mrs. Haviland kept up the pretense of having a "lovely evening" until the last guest had left the dining room, though Robin knew the old woman's heart was aching.

"Oh dear, oh dear," she said, more to herself than to Robin.

She was still seated at the head of the table, where dessert plates and coffee cups remained. As Ardith appeared in the doorway to remove them, Robin shook her head slightly and Ardith retreated.

"Oh dear." Tears began to well in Mrs. Haviland's eyes.

Robin moved quickly to the chair beside her and took hold of the wrinkled hand, which tonight felt especially cold and fragile. "Don't worry, Miss Emily. Greg loves you very much."

"But I wanted everything to be perfect for him and…and for you. Our guests don't usually speak so…graphically."

"It wouldn't have mattered if they hadn't. Greg was prepared to be obstinate when he walked through the door. I could tell by the set of his jaw. Please don't worry. His words had nothing to do with you personally." Now Robin's jaw was set. *I'll make damn sure he treats her with extra kindness tomorrow!*

"I know, but still…."

"I have an idea. Why don't you plan a gathering and invite people whom Greg would enjoy talking with and who would like to meet him. He's quite famous in his field, you know. There are plenty of excellent local artists and photographers—I'll bet they'd be thrilled to get an invitation."

The old woman's eyes brightened. "What a lovely idea! Why, there's Gary Fortson—he's a wonderful photographer and that Mr. Bricker who photographs historic buildings—can't think of his given name just now. Oh, and that young artist at the county high school who just won a national award for her painting of an owl. I'm sure her parents would come and bring her with them."

As Mrs. Haviland continued to think of guests, Robin relaxed in her chair. It was a good idea, and Greg would enjoy it. *That's another thing I'll make damn sure of!*

~~~

At ten o'clock the next morning Cassie rang Robin's doorbell, waking her from a deep sleep.

"What a slug-a-bed!" Cassie teased. "But I'm glad you were able to sleep so late. You've been needing it."

"Actually, I didn't get to sleep until sometime after three-thirty."

"Mama said the dinner didn't end very well last night."

"That's an understatement. It ended in a mess!" She sat down on the sofa, and Cassie eased her bulky, pregnant form down beside her. "I like Greg, Cassie. I really do," Robin said. "I've known him forever. He's a good friend, and I respect his work and his views. Why can't he respect mine?" She sighed in exasperation. "We're completely at odds!"

Cassie suppressed a smile. "Here's your mail," she said, changing the subject. "I went to the post office this morning."

Robin leafed through the bills and the "auto-sorts," tossing them onto the coffee table. There were a few sympathy cards and a letter for Patrick…from Ireland. She stared at it in disbelief, then ripped it open.

"What's wrong?" Cassie asked.

"I don't know anyone in Ireland. I didn't think Patrick did either, at least not after all the years he's been away." She scanned the letter quickly.

11 October
Dear Mr. Reilly:
This is to inform you of the passing of Mr. Ronan Reilly of Ballylith in County Kerry, Ireland, on 9 October. At his request, there was no funeral. He was buried in the family cemetery. Also, at his request, I am notifying you after the burial.

It is my understanding that you had planned to visit Ireland next month. Please don't change your plans because of Ronan Reilly's death. It is now even more urgent that you visit my office.
Yours truly,
Kern O'Sullivan, Solicitor
Tralee, Ireland

She stared at the letter for several seconds as an invasive, loathsome word crept into her mind and snaked slowly through her body—worming its way ·from the core of her being to the tips of her fingers and toes to the follicles of hair on her head—encroaching on all of the good thoughts she'd ever had…Deceived!

Robin's fragile grief now included her beloved Patrick's deceit.

It was just the beginning.

CHAPTER 5

Robin handed the letter to Cassie then leaned against the back of the sofa. Her heart was beating wildly.

"Are you all right?" Cassie asked, ever the nurse. She put a hand on Robin's forehead. "Just take it easy. Breathe slowly."

Robin waved her away. "Read that," she said, a little too sharply.

In a moment Cassie asked, "Who's Ronan Reilly?"

"I have no idea."

"Ever heard of Kern O'Sullivan?"

"Never. And County Kerry is *not* in Northern Ireland. Even I know that." Tears burned against her eyelids as she squeezed them shut. "Our family was supposed to have come from Ulster—*Northern* Ireland."

Cassie pulled some tissues from the dispenser on the table and put them into Robin's hands. *Just one more thing*, she thought. *One more problem she doesn't need!* "Dry your eyes and I'll pour you some wine," she said, rising, "then we'll talk about this."

Robin felt like screaming. She looked at the letter again: October 9. Ronan Reilly died on the ninth of October, two days *before* Patrick's death. And he didn't want Patrick notified until after his funeral—no, after the burial. *Oh, dear God!*

Cassie handed Robin a glass of port. "Sorry I can't join you in the wine," she said, patting her tummy, "but I'd rather be safe." She had poured a glass of water for herself.

"I don't understand this at all," Robin said. "Not any of it! Do you realize that this Ronan Reilly, whoever he is, died just two days ahead of Patrick? And this person, this Kern O'Sullivan, apparently knew that Patrick was going to Ireland next month, which is more than I knew, because I didn't know *when* he was going!" She gulped her wine.

"Well," Cassie said, glancing again at the letter, "it says here that Ronan Reilly was buried in the family cemetery. Seems to me that you have, or had, some family in Ireland after all, probably more closely related than you thought."

"But the Republic of Ireland? The southern part of the country?"
Cassie shrugged helplessly.

"Oh, Cassie," Robin whispered. "Why didn't I know?"

"Another thing," Cassie said. "Judging from the way Patrick shied away from talking about his family and from this sentence that says Patrick wasn't to be notified until after the burial, I'd guess that things might not have been too smooth between him and this Ronan person. Maybe Patrick had more than one reason for leaving. Maybe besides following his dream—I hate to say this, but—could he have been running from something?"

"What? And why? And why not tell me? I'm his daughter, for heaven's sake. I'm involved, too." Robin refilled her glass and took a long, slow sip. "What about my mother? Was she involved in this deception? I always thought she was so *honest*."

"Robin, please don't—"

"Cassie, do you suppose...do you suppose that Ronan Reilly might have been my...my grandfather?"

"There's a way of finding out." She glanced at her watch. "What time would it be in Ireland right now?"

"Oh, I don't know. I think they're four or five hours ahead of us."

"That makes it mid-afternoon over there. Call this Kern O'Sullivan and ask him. The number's right here," she said, pointing, "at the top of his fancy stationery."

Robin picked up the letter and started toward the phone in the kitchen. She was nervous. Scared stiff, in fact. Cassie followed her and sat at the table as Robin placed the call. It took time, but she finally got through to a secretary, who was equally difficult to get through. Eventually, Mr. O'Sullivan came on the line.

"It's Robin Reilly, is it?" he asked.

"Patrick Reilly's daughter, Mr. O'Sullivan."

"Yes, I know who you are."

"I'm glad because I didn't know who you were until thirty minutes ago." Her nervousness had miraculously disappeared, and there was silence at the other end of the line. "My father is dead," she finished.

"I am sorry to hear that, truly. Would you care to tell me about it?"

"It was an accident, on October eleventh, the same day you wrote your letter to him."

"I see. And what can I be doing for you, Miss Reilly?"

38

"You can tell me why my father felt it necessary to visit Ireland in November and why you felt it urgent that he visit your office." She took a deep breath. "And you can tell me who Ronan Reilly was."

"Ah," he spoke with a sigh. "You don't know then."

"Don't know *what*?"

"I'm afraid I am not at liberty to say."

Robin had to bite her tongue. "Mr. O'Sullivan, I'm beginning to get angry. I deserve some answers."

"I'm in complete agreement, Miss, but I am bound by legalities. May I suggest, if at all possible, that you be coming to Ireland and to my office, in your father's place."

Robin took a deep breath. "Tell me one thing, Mr. O'Sullivan. Was Ronan Reilly my grandfather?"

"No, miss, he was not."

"I see. Then for what good reason would I be going to Ireland?"

Cassie stifled a giggle. Robin had slipped into the lilt of the Irish. Just like that. She sounded so much like Patrick!

"I am holding a package that may be of great interest to you."

"Oh, for heaven's sake! Can't you just mail it to me?"

"That's not possible, miss."

"Legalities?"

"Exactly. You either come here to claim it, or you don't."

"And if I don't?"

"I think you should."

"*Damn* it, but you're exasperating! Well, I'll tell you something, Mr. Kern O'Sullivan. I'm coming to Ireland, and I'm coming to your office, and I'm going to get some answers to a whole lot of questions!" Robin slammed down the receiver.

~~~

Kern O'Sullivan heard the click and laughed aloud. *She's a Reilly all right*, he thought. *There'll be no doubt about that!*

~~~

Along the east wing of the Big House was a glassed-in loggia, which led to an indoor swimming pool at the far end. The pool, a favorite gathering place of plantation guests in the 1920s, was now drained of its "sulfur water" and closed, probably forever. The loggia, however, was decorated with potted palms and ficus and had several benches along its length, where one could sit and look out at the lake and the giant camphor tree in the distance. On the long wall behind the benches hung beautifully framed wildlife photographs by Greg Haviland.

There were two doors in the wall. The first led to a trophy room established in the late 1800s, trophies for field trials, hunting, shooting, and marksmanship. Several of the recent ones belonged to Robin.

The second door opened into a large room that had been converted to workspace for Greg's use, whenever he was home. It included a partitioned-off darkroom, where he was now developing what he felt was some of his finest work, not only the quail photos but also miscellaneous shots around the plantation. There was a particularly good one of Max, frozen in point, and one of Robin, taken unaware. Her hair was lifted slightly by the breeze, and the look on her face was one of intense pleasure. It was a beautiful photograph of a beautiful woman. Greg studied it as he hung it to dry. She was every bit as lovely in that bulky hunting gear as in the silk dress. Maybe even more so.

He had tried to endure last evening's table conversation. He really had tried, mostly for his grandmother's sake, but also for Robin's. But there came a point when he simply could not take any more. It went against everything he believed about compassion for living things. He picked up his photo of a mother quail, taken through the underbrush. *How could anyone,* he wondered, *take pleasure in making that beautiful creature "fold like a dishrag?"* He felt disgust. Yet, when he thought of Robin, her competence, and her obvious sincerity, his feeling was entirely different. She was different. She was kind and caring. He had seen that, when she helped him get the quail photos. He looked at the image of the flying covey, hanging from clips above his work table. *But,* he thought, *if Robin had been alone, she would have shot them dead. Oh, hell! Why should I care? None of this means one damn thing to me!* Greg stormed out of the room in search of his tennis racket. He'd drive to the club and slam a few balls around. He sure needed to slam something!

~~~

After Cassie left, Robin called Mr. Durbin about changing her vacation, which was scheduled for December, so that she could go to Ireland immediately, but there was no way he could spare her just now. With so many employees taking late vacations this year, it would be toward the end of November before she could go. That reminded her of Patrick's plans. Could he have left an airline ticket somewhere?

With a strange sense of intrusion, she opened the door to his bedroom, the first time she had stepped inside in several years. It was a large room, and even when Patrick was alive, it was an odd-looking room, mostly because of his choice and placement of furniture. His choice, not Anna's. She'd often said she would never furnish a room that way, but then she'd laugh and say it was the *only* room in the house that she let Patrick furnish and arrange. Now, the room seemed very odd indeed. The floor was covered with a natural jute rug, and right in the center of it sat the bed, angled diagonally to line up with the corner fireplace. One could walk all the way around the bed. As a child, Robin had *run* around it, playing chase with Anna. The walls, sponge-painted for texture, were adorned with mounted game—fish, birds, a deer head, and a rattlesnake. As a child, Robin had always felt comfortable here, especially on a cool winter's night when a low-burning fire warmed the room, and Patrick's whimsical stories and Anna's Irish songs warmed her heart. She would sit at the foot of the bed or in the small rocker near the hearth and feel she was in heaven. Now, the room was cold and lifeless and in need of airing. And she wondered if she had ever known Patrick Reilly. Really known him.

She felt guilty going through his things though there wasn't much she hadn't seen before—his clothing and accessories, a modest amount of jewelry, nothing terribly expensive. The airline ticket she sought was fairly accessible, in the top drawer of his dresser, shoved beneath rolls of socks. There was an envelope of cash there, too, nearly two thousand dollars. And a map of Ireland, which some travel company had marked with routes from Shannon Airport to Tralee.

Robin sat on the edge of the bed and looked closely at the map. The letter had said that Ronan Reilly died in Ballylith. But where was Ballylith? Her finger moved back and forth across County Kerry. *Ah, there it is!* Southeast of Tralee, along the River Feale. Tiny little place according to the map. No more than a village. Patrick didn't have it marked, and that was understandable. If he had come from County Kerry, rather than Northern Ireland, he was probably as familiar with that countryside as he was with the several-thousand acres of Haviland Plantation. But having major routes marked made sense. Much would have changed in the thirty-three years he'd been gone. *I was almost two years old then,* Robin thought. *Why can't I remember anything about it? Anything!*

41

She took a quick survey of the room, the closet, the adjoining small bathroom. All of Anna's belongings had been removed after her death. Aside from a collection of Irish songs and a book titled *The Irish Question*, which appeared to be about the centuries-old conflict between Northern Ireland and the Republic of Ireland, there was nothing to suggest that Patrick Brannigan Reilly had ever been anything other than a U.S. Southerner with an Irish name.

Robin took the airline ticket and the cash to her own room, noted the departure date as November 24, and made arrangements with Mr. Durbin to begin her vacation at that time. Five weeks to wait. She would miss Thanksgiving at the plantation, but it couldn't be helped.

~~~

That evening she went to Cassie and Jerome Davis's cottage for a supper of red beans and rice. Jerome met her on the wide front porch with his winning smile and a quick hug, and she was glad she had accepted their invitation. They were a remarkable couple—an example of the new generation of plantation workers. Cassie, of course, worked at the hospital rather than on the plantation; but Jerome, who had a degree in landscape architecture, supervised the immense grounds. His talents were well compensated, and his long-range plan was to open a landscaping business. He was a tall, handsome black man with a lot of faith in the future.

"Cassie tells me you're going to Ireland," he said, as they settled around the table.

Robin nodded. "On November twenty-fourth. I wish it could be sooner, but there's no possibility of getting away from my job before then."

"That's not so bad," said Cassie, passing the rice. "It will give you time to get yourself together, make plans, think."

"I'm not sure I want to think. My thoughts aren't very good right now."

"Robin," Jerome said, reaching to put a comforting hand on her arm, "spend some time remembering the Patrick you knew. Go back over your childhood, over your teen years, your college years. Think about all the time he spent with you because he *wanted* to and about the pride he took in your accomplishments. He was a good father, Robin. Don't take that away from him."

"I won't," Robin said softly. "I can't. And don't you make me cry in my beans, Jerome Davis." Jerome smiled. "If he'd just talked to me about the family," she continued. "If I didn't feel so…cheated; if I just *knew!*"

42

"If, if, if," Cassie injected. "And what did Patrick tell you about the 'ifs' in life? 'Accept them as they are or change them.' That's what he told me when I was ten years old, dreaming of becoming a nurse. You've already made plans to change things. You *are* going to find out about your family."

"But," said Jerome, "you also need to accept the fact that Patrick chose not to tell you, then forgive him for it. Maybe he was protecting you."

"You think I may not like what I'll find?"

"It's possible."

Robin thought a moment. "I still want to know," she said, finally.

"Then go for it."

CHAPTER 6

Late that night, Greg stood at the foot of the wrought iron stairs that circled up to Robin's home above the garage. He had seen her Ford compact tucked away for the night and was hoping she would still be up, so he could apologize for being so abrupt at his grandmother's dinner. But her lights were out. He considered tossing a pebble at her window like they did in old movies, but he didn't know which window, and he didn't want to frighten her. God knows he might find himself staring into the wrong end of a rifle!

He had told himself for two days that it didn't matter what she thought of him. But it did. Maybe it was because they had been childhood friends; maybe it was because he wanted to please his grandmother; maybe it was because Robin was special.

The apology will have to wait, he thought, turning back toward the Big House. He would be flying to New York in the morning and wouldn't be back for five days.

~~~

Robin lay awake, not even trying to sleep. There was too much to think about, including Wednesday night's disaster, but there simply hadn't been a good time to approach Greg about it. Besides, she wouldn't have known what to say. She still felt no need to apologize, yet she didn't want him to think badly of her. Maybe it was because they had been childhood friends; maybe it was because she wanted to please his grandmother; maybe it was because she cared about him in a special way. *As for anything more, we're not the same type by a long shot*! Though the unintentional pun was only in her mind, it made her laugh aloud.

~~~

The next day, after mass at St. Margaret's in Monticello, Robin drove directly to the Big House to visit with Miss Emily, as was often her custom.

45

She walked around back to the terrace, knowing she would find the lady of the house stretched out on her wicker *chaise longue* with a novel in her hands.

"Oh, Robin, dear, pull up a chair," said Mrs. Haviland. "I am so glad you've come!" She put a marker in her book, adding, "You *must* read this when I've finished. It's very exciting!" Her voice was musical and her eyes twinkled. Robin adored her.

"Is it Agatha Christie?" she asked.

"No, dear. It's Peter Lovesey. Very British and very up-to-date! The story takes place in Bath, England, among all those Roman ruins." She lifted the little silver bell and shook it, but Ardith had anticipated her and was just arriving with two iced teas. "I've been working on plans for our little *soirée*," she said after Ardith had gone. "It's such a wonderful idea! But I'm afraid it will be a few weeks before I can get everyone together—the guests I want, that is. Gary Fortson and his wife are away on vacation right now. He's a marvelous photographer, won some prizes locally, I understand; and his wife is an absolutely delightful person to be around. They are a *must* for our gathering." She stopped for a sip of tea. "Have you spoken to Greg since Wednesday evening, dear?"

Robin shook her head. "No, I'm afraid not. We just haven't run into each other. Is he here now?"

"Oh, no, dear. He's gone to New York."

Robin felt her heart sink, and the feeling surprised her. "I thought he was going to stay a while," she said.

Miss Emily nodded enthusiastically. "Through Christmas, actually. It will be the longest he's stayed on the plantation since he was a child. He'll be back in a few days," she added. "Do try to speak with him, Robin. He's been very pleasant to me, but I still feel uneasy about what happened at dinner that night."

Robin patted the wrinkled arm. "I will speak to him because I am uneasy, too; but don't worry about Greg. He's a good person, and he would never let a few moments of dinner conversation come between him and his beloved grandmother." Robin reached for the pitcher. "May I refill your glass?" she asked.

"Just a tad, dear. Just a tad."

"Miss Emily, I…uh, I'd like to ask you something, and I hope you'll give me an honest answer."

The lady considered that. "Let's say, if I cannot give you an honest answer, I won't answer you at all."

Robin grinned. "If that's the best you can do, I'll take it." She refilled her own glass. "Did Patrick ever give you any indication that we had relatives still living in Ireland?"

"No."

"Please think carefully. Think back thirty years or more. I know you have an excellent memory, and you've told me many times that you were the one who decided to hire Patrick. What did he tell you about himself when he applied for the job?"

"Hmmm...." She lifted a finger to her cheek, as though the simple gesture would aid her thinking. "He said that he and Anna had saved their money to emigrate because there was no opportunity left in Ireland. Income was low, and the unemployment rate was high and going up. 'Dreams only linger there,' he said. I was very impressed with his way of speaking and his good manners, and my late husband was impressed with his knowledge of mechanical things. That combination made him an excellent choice for the plantation."

Robin waited while Mrs. Haviland thought some more.

"One interesting thing I remember him saying was, 'In Ireland, folks are either younger than fifteen or older than sixty-five.' That stuck in my mind. Patrick and Anna would have been in their early thirties then."

"That's right. He would have been sixty-eight this year."

"One can't blame them for wanting to get away. No young couples their own age. He said that leaving Ireland at that time became known as 'the habit.' 'Tis the habit they've got,' he said."

"Did he say where in Ireland they came from?"

"Oh, definitely Northern Ireland, dear. Patrick was employed as an industrial mechanic there. I wish I could name the company, but it was a funny-sounding name, and it just didn't stick with me. I'm sorry."

"Probably a Gaelic name. Why are you so sure he came from Northern Ireland?"

"Well, because he said so. That's where most industry was located at that time. The Republic of Ireland was nearly all agricultural. That I remember from newspaper reports. That was the time of that terrible uprising, you know, 1969, and it was in all the papers for weeks on end."

"Did he say what city they lived in?"

"My goodness, Robin, didn't he tell you *anything*?"

"He did, but I'd like to hear it from you. Maybe there's something he forgot to tell me."

This time Mrs. Haviland patted Robin's arm. "Of course, dear," she said, indulgently. "They lived in Belfast. That was until sometime in the fall of .1969. They came here with you in early December. Patrick said they'd been planning to leave the country for a long time, but they couldn't make the move until after the British troops came in and settled things down. That gave them one more good excuse to leave. 'When the troops came in, we went out,' he said."

"Did he ever say anything about the Republic? About County Kerry?"

The lady again sipped her tea and considered. "No," she said, finally. "Nothing about the south of Ireland, other than traveling there. He mentioned driving through Limerick and Cork, and, oh, he said he'd like to take *me* for a ride in a donkey cart around the Lakes of Killarney. Imagine! I told him I was sure he had included a visit to the Blarney Stone in his travels!" She chuckled. "'For sure 'n I've kissed it many a time,' he said."

Robin laughed. Miss Emily's imitation of the "lilt" was pretty darned good. "Did he...did he ever mention someone named Ronan Reilly?"

Mrs. Haviland looked puzzled. "I gather this is important to you."

"Very."

She shook her head and sighed. "I'm sorry," she said. "I've never heard of Ronan Reilly." It was an honest answer.

Robin had learned precious little. Apparently, Patrick had told his employer the same stories—lies!—he had told his daughter.

CHAPTER 7

During the next week on the job, Robin's department was the busiest in the company, or at least appeared to be. The assistants who had slacked off in her absence now huffed and puffed to keep up with her demands. When they complained, she snapped, "Take aerobics classes," or "Quit whining and do your job!" Robin Reilly had become a terror, and subordinates and co-workers alike gave her plenty of space. She was trying to keep her sanity for four more weeks, the longest four weeks of her life. Fortunately, her co-workers gave her a wide path and a lot of understanding.

She didn't go back to the plantation until Saturday, and when she arrived, there was a message from Greg stuck to her door. She tore it off and read as she entered the loft. He wanted to take her to dinner that evening. Her first thoughts were, *I'm not up to this. I don't feel like an evening of apologies. I'd rather break something!* It was obvious, even to her, that her nerves were prickling her from the inside out. She felt like a cat with a fur ball.

She took a deep breath, then another, then closed her eyes and "listened" to Patrick. *Ah, Robin, me girl, go out with Greg and have yourself a fine time. Sooner or later ye'll have to pull the weeds out of that friendship, you know.*

She sighed. "It's true," she said aloud, adding, as she opened her eyes, "though I don't know why I should listen to you, Patrick Reilly! You've left me nothing but a pile o' trouble!"

Nevertheless, she accepted the invitation, dressing carefully but casually in a royal blue sweater and skirt with gold jewelry, for they were going to a very special tavern, which, Greg said, was the closest thing he could find to an Irish pub. She knew the place well. It was a cozy little room in the basement of a nineteenth-century house just north of Monticello, over the Georgia line.

As they stepped inside onto the cool brick floor, the scents and sounds of sizzling stirfry enveloped them.

"Ummm," Robin murmured appreciatively. She couldn't help it.

Multifaceted lights sparkled from exposed beams overhead, and huge pieces of original artwork softened the dark wood walls. In the far corner a small combo played dance tunes—not Irish, but good just the same.

"So why did you dash off to New York?" Robin asked after they'd ordered.

"I needed to meet with my editor. She keeps me focused."

"What's the project? Or can't you tell me?"

He smiled. "It's what the advertising world refers to as a coffee table book."

"Why, that's exciting, Greg! Is it your first book?"

"Not exactly. But it's my first *good* book. And you're right. It is exciting. That's why I want to stay on target and do it well."

"Will the quail be in it?"

"Of course. And Max."

Robin laughed. "I won't dare show it to Max. He already thinks he's the best-looking dog in the kennel!"

They discussed Greg's book until the food arrived—potato skins, fried cheese sticks, bean soup, and huge hamburgers. When the waiter had gone, they both said, simultaneously, "About last Wednesday—"

"You first," Robin offered.

Greg looked her straight in the eye. "I apologize for my behavior," he said.

"You don't need to apologize, Greg."

"Yes, I do, if for no other reason than good manners. If anyone was ever taught the social graces while growing up, I certainly was. There are more subtle—and definitely more acceptable—ways to leave a gathering. My views, however, I cannot apologize for," he added.

"Good. I can't apologize for mine either, but I am sorry that our differences keep getting between us." His eyes were dark, almost black, penetrating. Nervously, she looked away as the musicians slid into a different song, then turned back. "Could we just accept each other as we are and build from there?"

He lifted his glass and nodded, his smile sparkling. "I'm glad you added the 'building' part," he said.

For the first time in the last several days, she looked at him, *really* looked at him—his sharply defined features, his strong chin, his thick dark hair, his athletic build. She watched him sip his wine.

"Gran says you were asking some pretty serious questions," he said.

Robin blinked then took a bite of fried cheese to mask her slight blush.

"About Ireland," he added.

After a quick swallow of ice water, she removed Kern O'Sullivan's letter from her pocket and handed it over. "I was hoping I'd have the opportunity to show this to you. So far, Cassie and Jerome are the only ones who know about it, except for Mr. Durbin. And all he knows is that I'm going to Ireland next month."

"You're going to Ireland?" Greg quickly read the letter. "Have you called this O'Sullivan?"

She nodded. "His favorite word is 'legalities.' He can't tell me anything because of legalities. But he did say that he had a package for me, and I gathered from what he said that I had to go to his office to get it."

"What did he say, exactly?"

Robin didn't have to consider that one. The words had been burned into her brain. "'You either come here to claim it, or you don't,' he said. 'And if I don't?' I asked. All he answered was, 'I think you should.'"

"Sounds to me like he's bound by stipulations in a will. Do you know who this Ronan Reilly was?"

She shook her head. "I asked Mr. O'Sullivan if he were my grandfather, and he said no. That's all I know about any of this. Patrick had told me that we were from Northern Ireland, but this letter comes from the South, from the Republic of Ireland. And I've never in my life heard of a place called Ballylith."

"Was Gran any help?"

"She'd been told the same stories I had—lies!"

"You don't have any choice, then, do you?"

"Not really. It's all I've thought about since last Thursday. I found Patrick's plane ticket, and I'm going to use it."

"I wish there were something I could say that would help you."

She smiled. "Just listening helps. It's not the kind of thing I want the world to know—my father lied to me—but it's a relief to share it with someone I trust."

Greg swallowed hard, feeling somewhat guilty. She trusted him. But *he had* heard of Ballylith from Patrick's own mouth. In order to tell Robin, he would also have to tell her that Patrick was stone drunk at the time. Patrick *never* drank, but Greg had found him lying on the ground one night near the lake, babbling about Ireland.

"Sure 'n ye found me, lad," he'd said when Greg sat him up. "But don't be tellin'. Gi' me yer promise?"

And he did. Patrick was truly pitiful. Greg took him to the loft and put him to bed, thankful that Robin was staying in Tallahassee. He'd never told anyone, least of all his grandmother. She loved her blackberry wine and liqueur, but anything else was strictly forbidden on the plantation. Or, as Berry might have put it, "Miss Emily'd have a conniption!"

When Patrick had mentioned Ballylith, Greg supposed it was a slurring of something else by Patrick's nearly immobile tongue, and that his talk of "those Reillys at the castle" was the result of a muddled mind. Now he wasn't so sure.

Obsession. That was the word! Robin had said that Patrick's trip to Ireland had become *an obsession.* He yearned to go back. That had bothered Greg at the time, but he hadn't connected it. He had had the same feeling the night he found Patrick. Obsession with things in Ireland that Greg had no way of understanding, especially in the throes of Patrick's confusion. Nothing made sense. Finally, Patrick had given up. "Forget it, lad. I don't mean diddly," Patrick had said as he closed his eyes and began to snore.

Well, Greg thought, studying Robin's face across the table. *I'm going to honor my promise to Patrick. He doesn't need another mark against his name. Patrick Reilly was a good man, damn it all to hell! If there are Reillys living in a castle in Ballylith, they won't be any better than Patrick was, and Robin will know that soon enough.*

~~~

The following weekend Robin found the letters. They were in a shoebox in the bottom of Patrick's closet, which she had been cleaning. She had lifted out the seldom-worn shoes to put aside for Goodwill, and there the Irish postmarks lay, staring up at her. Carefully, she lifted them out and took them to the bed in the center of the room. They were arranged in order, the first postmarked 1982.

5 December
Dear Patrick,
Maeve and I were distressed to learn of Anna's death. But you're a true Irishman, Patrick. You'll cope.
Sincerely,
Ronan

"You'll cope." Robin had heard that line before, but coping was becoming increasingly hard to do. Now there was a Maeve. Maeve Reilly?

The next was mailed in 1984.

14 May
Dear Patrick,
This is to inform you of Maeve's death last month. The other is fine.
Sincerely,
Ronan

The other is fine? The other *what*? Robin's hands were beginning to tremble. The man certainly didn't believe in long letters!

Four years later:

28 December
Dear Patrick,
Today is the coming of age. A package has been left with the O'Sullivan firm in Tralee.
Should anything happen to me, please see that it is claimed.
Sincerely,
Ronan

Robin read it again. *The coming of age*, she thought, looking once more at the date. *Why, that's my birthday! In—that would be, let's see, 1988— it was my...my twenty-first birthday*! She reached quickly for the last letter. The handwriting was different. A feminine hand. And the envelope was postmarked just six weeks ago!

20 September
Dear Mr. Patrick,
I know I shouldn't be writing this letter, but I'm too worried not to. Mr. Ronan's health is failing, and it's almost more than I can do to handle the both of them, though I've served thirty-four years in this home. I was told not to contact you, but that just don't seem right. Won't you please come to visit him in his last days? Maybe you can persuade him to change his mind about Wrenny.
Sincerely,
Gilda Lynch
(Housekeeper)

~~~

Near dawn the next morning Robin's recurring dream jolted her from a drugged sleep. She had been hiding under something, with someone. They were watching a fire, feeling the heat, hearing the snap of flames. There was noise, the sound of running feet, then a loud bang and a bright light! Robin screamed—but this time it wasn't silent. She was crying out loud, over and over again, "Wrenny! Wrenny! Wrenyyyyy!"

She awoke, gasping for breath.

Oh, God! Who is Wrenny?

CHAPTER 8

Greg heard the screams as he passed by the garage on his way to the woods. Very quickly he ran to the stairs, taking them two at a time. He dropped his equipment bag on the foyer floor, ringing the bell with one hand, banging on the door with the other. By then the screaming had stopped.

"Robin! Robin, what's wrong? Can you come to the door? Answer me or I'll break it in!"

"C-coming! Don't…don't break it!" She reached for her terry wrapper and stepped into her slippers. She was still shaking, and breathing was difficult, but she felt great relief at being awake. A glance in the mirror showed disheveled hair and a mottled complexion, but she didn't care. She was very glad that Greg had come.

In the living room she turned on a table lamp before hurrying to open the door. It was barely dawn.

"Greg," she said, clutching his hand, pulling him inside. "I've remembered something!"

"What happened? You scared the hell out of me. Again! I thought someone was attacking you."

She moved quickly to the sofa, urging him to sit beside her. "It's a dream. A nightmare! I've had a recurring nightmare since I was a child—this is the seventh time it's happened—and each time I wake up trying to scream someone's name, but I never remember the name and the screaming has always been *silent*—terribly frightening, screaming with nothing coming out…until now. Greg, I woke up screaming aloud!"

"No kidding. You were probably heard in downtown Monticello!"

"Don't you see? It was the name in Gilda Lynch's letter—Wrenny. That's the name that's been missing all these years!"

"You've lost me. Who is Gilda Lynch?"

"Oh, sorry. Wait just a minute." She hurried to her bedroom and retrieved the letters. "Read these," she said, thrusting them into his hands. She sat close, peering over his arm as he read. "I found them yesterday in Patrick's closet."

55

As Greg finished the last letter, he asked, "Who is Wrenny? Do you know?"

She shook her head. "No, I don't, but I'm certain now that the dream is real, that it's something that actually happened to me when I was a child. Wrenny was probably a playmate. In the dream we were hiding, and terrible things were going on around us—fire, shouting, running, shooting!"

"Robin," Greg said slowly, taking her hands in his. "Think about that for just a minute."

Robin's look questioned him.

"If it did happen, you must have been in Northern Ireland during the 1969 uprising. And if I remember my history, it happened in the fall of that year. When did you come here?"

"In early December 1969. I was almost two years old."

"So maybe Patrick didn't lie after all."

She sighed heavily. "I'm inclined to think now that he didn't lie, but I also think he left out an awful lot of truth. Oh, Greg, my comfortable routine life has been uprooted, shaken unmercifully and thrown back onto the ground. I'll never be a complete person until it's firmly planted again!" Very suddenly and against her will, she started to cry.

Greg put his arm around her and pulled her close to his body. He was warm and strong, and she felt good there, leaning against him until the tears and the shaking subsided. Even then she didn't move away. She didn't want to.

He held her tightly for a long time then began stroking her hair. She smelled of sleep and good shampoo, and he lowered his face to her brow, kissing her lightly above the eyes. The closeness sent a surge of warmth throughout his body, and he knew then that Robin Reilly would somehow make a mark on his life. For good or bad, she would be important to him. In all of his years he had never felt quite like that about anyone.

After a while she moved away. "I'm scared, Greg," she said. "I'm scared half to death of going to Ireland...but I'm even more frightened of *not* going."

"Would you like me to go with you?" he asked softly.

Her face, wet with tears, was suddenly transformed, first by astonishment, then by utter joy. "Would you?" she whispered.

More than anything in the world, he wanted to kiss her, *really* kiss her, but all he could do was nod and smile. The moment was too fragile for more.

~~~

Cassie was seated comfortably in the rocker by the hearth in Berry's kitchen at the Big House. Everyone thought of it as Berry's kitchen. Her mother was rolling out pastry for pecan tarts, which the hunters would enjoy for tonight's dessert. Oyster stew bubbled on the stove.

"I think it's wonderful, Robin goin' to Ireland," Berry said. "It's time she saw where she be born."

"I think so, too. Someday," Cassie added, wistfully, "Jerome and I are going to travel."

"Where to?"

"Oh, I don't know. All kinds of exotic places."

"Exotic places?" Berry chuckled, and her body shook. "Honey chile, I can go right across the line to Georgia and go to Rome, Athens, Berlin and Cairo—'cept in Georgia they call it Kayro. And if I wants to go to Ireland, there's Dublin, too. Oh, an' don' forgit Shannon, up in the mountains where yo' Uncle Jess lives."

Cassie laughed aloud. "Mama, you're a mess!"

"Go taste the stew," Berry said. "See if it's right."

"You know it's perfect," Cassie replied, still smiling. She pushed herself out of the chair. "You just want a compliment."

Mrs. Haviland appeared at the kitchen door. "This sounds like a happy place to rest for a few minutes," she said. She moved to the hearth and sat delicately in one of the rockers. "And it smells good, too," she added.

"Tastes as good as it smells," Cassie said, putting her spoon in the sink. She returned to the other rocker. "Mama eats up compliments, you know. She'd rather have them than food."

"Oh, go on with you!" Berry said, grinning.

"When is your baby due, Cassie?" asked Mrs. Haviland. "I know it's December, but I can't seem to remember the date."

"The twelfth, just after Robin and Greg return from Ireland."

"Now I, for one, sho am glad that young man be goin' with her," said Berry. "She don' need to be traipsin' off by herself so soon after her daddy's funeral, especially to the place where he come from. That be hard to take. Hard," she repeated, shaking her head.

"Just between us," said Mrs. Haviland, "I am glad Greg is going, too, though I'm not sure that it's proper."

Cassie suppressed a smile. "They'll be fine, ma'am. They're good people."

"Hmmm. I don't live in a vacuum, Cassie. I just hope nothing…well, happens." To herself, the lady hoped quite differently. She hoped something would indeed "happen" because she knew very well that Robin was the right young woman for her grandson, even if he could not see it himself. Outwardly, she straightened her skirt, which didn't need straightening, and grimaced for appearance's sake.

Berry and the rest of the plantation folk thought Robin was going to Ireland for a vacation, to see the country where she was born. Mrs. Haviland suspected there was more to it than that, but only Cassie and Jerome knew for sure.

~~~

For Robin, the next two weeks flew by. She stayed in Tallahassee, working days and shopping in the evenings. The clothing she wore in North Florida would not be adequate in Ireland, where the weather this time of year would be cold and wet and probably windy. She would need wool-blend slacks and skirts and some sweaters that were heavier than the soft cottons hanging in her closet. She really wasn't into "tweeds," but she suspected she would buy some in Ireland—maybe for Miss Emily—along with Irish lace and linen.

On the afternoon of November 22 (her last day at work), the office gang surprised her with a *bon voyage* celebration. They even had invited her ex-husband, Tripp Nicholson, because after seeing him with her at Patrick's funeral, they thought it would please her. She was very touched and a little chagrined since she had been such a tyrant with everyone these past weeks.

She had taken a late lunch—not to eat, but to do some last-minute shopping—and upon returning, was greeted with cheers and fluttering streamers of Irish green. One of the desks had been converted to a table by covering it with a sheet, which hung to the floor on all sides. In the center was a world globe with a small Republic of Ireland flag sticking up from the top. There were Irish goodies on the table—skewered chunks of cold smoked salmon, thin slices of "sweet bread," and a delicious lime-green punch. She was suddenly famished.

"Sorry we don't have Irish coffee," Jack Tanner whispered in her ear, "but old Durbin drew the line there. We'll have to get the stronger stuff after hours." Robin smiled and politely nodded her head, knowing full well there wouldn't be any "stronger stuff" for her. She intended to leave for the plantation immediately after work, for there was still much to do before Sunday's flight.

Tripp filled her punch cup and talked with her of trivial things. He'd started dating a law student at Florida State—a former Miss Florida, he noted—and seemed very pleased with himself. *She's really what Tripp needs,* Robin thought truthfully, without bitterness. *He needs something showy on his arm.*

After a time of socializing, Jack Tanner made a little speech and presented Robin with a going-away gift from all the staff. It was a travel kit filled with items she would need and would surely have forgotten, such as needle and thread, folding scissors, a small tube of hand lotion, a fold-up shopping bag.

"And now," said Mr. Durbin, who had arrived late, "you're to take the rest of the afternoon off. That's my gift." He smiled uncomfortably while everyone applauded.

Robin wanted to hug him, but she restrained herself. Mr. Durbin had moved to Florida from Ohio and wasn't a natural "hugger." He was nice but as stiff as parchment and would probably crack just as easily. "Thank you," she said, from the bottom of her heart. "Thank you all!"

~~~

Robin and Greg drove to the Tallahassee Airport early Sunday morning in Robin's Ford and parked the car in the long-term lot. No way would she allow Greg to leave his Jaguar there! She was grateful they would be flying by day, rather than on one of the more easily booked night flights, because she didn't want to sleep through anything! There was the relatively short flight to Atlanta, where they would have a change of planes then settle in for a seven-hour trip to Shannon, Ireland, aboard Delta Airlines.

Robin had been tense for weeks, and she'd been especially jumpy the last couple of days. Now, though, with the luggage checked onto the plane and Greg with her in the terminal, she felt strangely calm. She looked at him as he stood by the window, watching airport personnel prepare their plane. He was strong yet gentle, firm yet kind, and the most unusual blend of plain and fancy Robin had ever known. Why he had offered to come with her, she couldn't imagine, but she thanked the Holy Mother for him again and again. And just as she was thanking the Holy Mother one more time, they were called for boarding.

Greg picked up his camera bag and Robin's carry-on. "The adventure begins," he said with a smile. "Are you still nervous?"

"No," she said, returning his smile. "I'm terribly excited but not nervous. Not one bit nervous." And that was the truth. Robin Reilly was ready for whatever lay ahead.

PART II

IRELAND
NOVEMBER
THE PRESENT

CHAPTER 9

Given the time difference, it was 9:00 p.m. as their plane approached Shannon International Airport, so Robin and Greg didn't get to see Ireland from the air. And when they stepped from the plane onto Irish soil, the perpetual mist was so heavy that their first glimpse of the country amounted to little more than the terminal building.

They rented a car and drove to their hotel near the airport. Since it was still late afternoon back home (though pitch black in Ireland), they were both hungry.

"Let's just eat here in the hotel," Robin suggested. "It's dark and rainy anyway. We wouldn't be able to see anything."

"Do you realize that we'll have to get up at 3:00 a.m.—U.S. time—in order to keep the appointment with O'Sullivan in Tralee tomorrow?" Greg asked.

"You're kidding!"

"That's allowing an extra hour in case we get lost."

"With so little sleep, I'll be cranky during the meeting."

"Had you planned to be otherwise?"

She poked him playfully then looked down at her travel clothes as they entered the hotel restaurant. "I don't know about this," she said, shaking her head. Her clothes were crumpled and her hair felt ratty.

"Don't worry. You look—"

"I look what?"

"Like a tourist."

Robin giggled.

"We'd better order something that's easy on the stomach," Greg suggested. "And it would make sense to go to bed early."

"No problem. I'm already exhausted." *Separate rooms,* she thought, then sighed.

Separate rooms, thought Greg. I sure as hell hope we don't spend the whole trip in separate rooms!

~~~

Ireland's own George Bernard Shaw once said, "The Irish climate will make the stiffest and slowest mind flexible for life." Robin recalled that as they drove through the countryside the next morning. The weather was certainly unpredictable, and there was something in the air that made the time difference no difference at all. Whatever it was, it was exhilarating! She'd had a good night's sleep, however short, and now, it was a good thing she wasn't driving because she couldn't take her eyes away from the view. She didn't even want to blink!

They drove through some of the prettiest hilly country Robin had ever seen. Ireland was like a great green fairyland, just as Patrick had told her, like she'd read about as a child. The mist had lifted, and a rainbow had come and gone, leaving the moist ground sparkling in the sunlight and cool air. Here, it was easy to believe in leprechauns.

They crossed the River Shannon into Limerick, passing near "Durty Nellie's" famous pub and Bunratty Castle on the way.

"Before we leave Ireland," Greg said, "we're coming back here one evening."

"To the pub? Really?"

"To the castle. It's been restored as in medieval times. You'll like the food and the music. And I like the serving wenches," he added with a grin.

Robin stared. "You've been here before? You didn't tell me!"

"I haven't been to Tralee, and I've never heard of Ballylith (*God forgive one small lie*, he thought), but yes, I have visited some parts of Ireland."

"What parts?"

"Well, in addition to Limerick, I've been to Galway and Cork, and to Wexford and Dublin up the east coast. Sorry to say, I haven't visited many small towns." He glanced at her, thinking how beautiful she looked, but he said, "The road from Limerick to Tralee should be especially beautiful. The mountains get softer and softer as we go southwest."

"Softer, hmm? Patrick used that expression." Smiling, Robin settled back in the passenger's seat. They were following the route Patrick had marked on his map, from Limerick to Newcastle West, to Tralee. Greg was certain he could have devised a more efficient route, but Robin wanted to go Patrick's way. It probably had been familiar country to him many years ago, and she wanted to see it as he had.

Despite the hills and hairpin curves, the road was fairly good, though driving on the left side provided a thrill of its own. And how beautiful it was! Heather-clad mountains, patches of gorse, rhododendrons, clusters of quaint cottages, people on bicycles, and herds of sheep—even in the road! Each sheep had a little splotch of color on its hindquarters. Sort of like a dollop of paint.

Strangely, it seemed to Robin that the farther they traveled into County Kerry, the slower the people moved. There was a genuine sense of peace, something Robin had not expected. Truth was, she didn't know *what* to expect, but she could imagine Patrick in this setting. He would fit.

As they neared Tralee, they realized that they hadn't needed all of the extra hour Greg had allowed, so they stopped at a tiny, family-run restaurant for a cup of hot tea. It was here that Robin had her first taste of Ireland's coarse-textured soda bread, served warm with sweet butter.

"Greg," she asked as they ate, "have you ever been to Northern Ireland?"

"No," he answered. "Do you want to go there?"

"Oh, yes! If Mr. O'Sullivan can give me details, I want to see where I was born, where Patrick worked...what I might have become."

Greg covered her hand with his. "Had you stayed in Ireland, you might have acquired a lilt instead of a drawl, Robin Reilly, but I doubt that you would have been any different inside."

Robin considered that for a long moment. "I don't know how you meant that," she said, finally, "but I'm going to take it as a compliment. Now," she continued, rising, "let's go see that Mr. Kern O'Sullivan. He'll be having a lot o' questions to answer!" Her eyes had the Irish twinkle.

～～～

Kern O'Sullivan was a surprise. Robin had expected a bewhiskered little troll of a man who would remember the past, predict the future, and "remove all doubts and fears." Like God. What she got was a young Irishman with black curly hair and a quick wit, who knew only what was contained in the files he had inherited from his deceased grandfather. After introductions and requesting and inspecting Robin's identification, O'Sullivan invited them to be seated.

"So you're wanting the package," he began, settling himself behind his desk.

"No," said Robin, looking him straight in the eye. "I want to know what's *in* the package. Then I'll tell you if I want it."

Greg, sitting on a small sofa at the side, covered a grin with his hand. Robin's temper was a bit close to the surface.

The Irishman laughed. "Just like old Ronan, you are. I only met him once, but he gave me one devil of a time!"

"You can start by telling me who 'old Ronan' was. I'd never heard of him until your letter arrived. And why wouldn't you tell me over the phone?"

"Ronan Reilly's will stipulates two things: That either Patrick or yourself must be physically present in this office to hear what it contains—that's the 'package,' by the way—and that you not be told anything of your family. In other words, me girl, you should be sufficiently curious and mildly acquiescent, though I cannot imagine that you will be."

"I'm not your girl," Robin snapped. "And if you don't tell me who Ronan Reilly was, I don't want the damned package! It's clear to me now that he didn't care at all about me and not much more about Patrick, writing him three letters in thirty years!"

"I don't know why he kept silent, but I'm sure he had good reason," O'Sullivan said, tugging at his plaid tie. "Ronan Reilly was not a mean man. My grandfather could have told you more than I can, but he's been gone these last few years, God rest his soul." He crossed himself. "All I know for sure, and I don't see any reason for not telling you, is that Ronan Reilly was your great-uncle."

Robin sat back in her chair. It was the first piece of solid information she'd had since this whole thing began.

"Would you like me to tell you the gist o' the will?" O'Sullivan asked kindly.

Robin nodded.

"It's very simple, really. You inherit the bulk of his estate. *But,*" he said, holding up his hand, "don't be thinking you're a rich woman. Reilly Castle barely breaks even, and it's my advice to sell it if ye can find a body fool enough to buy."

Robin was dumbfounded. "Reilly *Castle?*"

"'Tis a small castle east of here in the village of Ballylith on the River Feale, not so much a castle as a country home. I believe it's been in the Reilly family since it was built some four hundred years ago. But these old places, you know, it's hard to keep them up, and there aren't many rich folks around any more who can hire their work done. The houses give in to damp rot and weather, and Reilly Castle is no exception. It may be better than some, though, for Ronan Reilly had the good sense to start taking in paying guests.

I understand it's a pretty fair bed-and-breakfast place, has three or four bedrooms fixed up decently for visitors."

"You've never been there."

"No. 'Twas never invited."

"I mean as a paying guest."

"Now why would I be going into the middle of nowhere? I'm a young man. I like action, not stagnation."

Greg cleared his throat. "Mr. O'Sullivan," he said, "who's been taking care of the property since Mr. Reilly's death?"

"Oh, 'tis well looked after, sir. Gilda Lynch, the housekeeper, is still there, and whenever guests are booked, she has a woman from the village come in and do the cooking. Then there's Fergus Halloran. He doesn't live there, but he goes three days a week to look after the grounds and take care of any odd jobs that need doing. That's all the hired help, I'm afraid. I told you, 'tis not a prosperous place."

He hadn't mentioned Wrenny. The housekeeper's letter had definitely said, *Maybe you can persuade him to change his mind about Wrenny.* "You're sure there's no one else living there?" Robin asked.

"Ah, well, and that's another wee problem." Kern O'Sullivan had a sheepish look on his face, and he sighed as he continued. "Wren Reilly lives there now, but she'll be gone soon. Old Ronan made it clear that she was to leave after his death and before you, or Patrick, arrived. That was one of the things he went on so about when he was here in this office, giving me that devil of a time I spoke of. Apparently he didn't want your paths to cross. But I'm afraid her accommodations won't be ready for another week yet." He lifted his arms in a grand shrug. "I tried," he said.

Robin's mouth was very dry. "Who is Wren Reilly?" she asked.

"Don't know."

"How old is she?"

"Don't know that either."

"Then I guess I'll just have to go to Reilly Castle and find out for myself, won't I?" said Robin as she rose, her heart pounding in her chest.

O'Sullivan stood. Greg was already on his feet.

"Look, I apologize for not having her out of there," said O'Sullivan. "My grandfather would have managed it somehow, but me, I'm busy, and well, it plain seemed silly to ask her to move twice."

Robin smiled for the first time since she'd entered the office. It was a sincere, sparkling smile that lit up her whole face and made her truly beautiful. "Oh, don't apologize, Mr. O'Sullivan. I'd say you've done everything exactly right."

~~~

The journey to Ballylith was arduous. Robin's mind was on Reilly Castle and what she might find there. Who was Wren Reilly? A cousin? Granddaughter of Great-Uncle Ronan? *Wrenny,* her companion in the dream. And why did Ronan ignore Robin in life then give her his estate in death? Or would that be "saddle" her with his estate, as Kern O'Sullivan had implied? This time, when sheep crossed the road holding up the scant traffic, they were a nuisance rather than a delight because Robin was impatient, even annoyed that the animals had the right-of-way. She didn't even look at the "Forty Shades of Green" in the fields or the hills of lavender heather.

Greg was worried. He had a feeling that whatever awaited Robin would not be a pleasure. He was familiar with the impoverished country homes of Irish landowners. Many were nearly impossible financial burdens for families to bear. Since most were originally second homes, the enormous capital taxes now forced the owners to live in them permanently, to farm the land, to grow barley, to raise sheep, or to take in paying guests. In essence, the master of the house became servant to it. If this awaited Robin, O'Sullivan was right—sell it, or as many owners had already done, walk away and let it rot. Not a very romantic solution but practical. As for Wren Reilly, Greg didn't even care to speculate.

As they followed the sign pointing to Ballylith, there were a few isolated farm houses, then some cottages, and finally, the village. Robin's eyes widened in surprise. Ballylith was the most quaint and picturesque place she had ever seen. No modern shopping centers or tall office buildings. The homes were thatch-roofed with bright-colored doors, and in every window were lace curtains. The few people walking about were dressed "sensibly" in tweeds, caps, and low-heeled shoes. The main street, lined with old-fashioned street lamps, ended abruptly at a "T" crossroad in front of a small, immaculately groomed Catholic church. Greg had to ask for directions to Reilly Castle, so he turned to the right, where a few yards up the road was a short, stout man selling farm goods from the back of a horse-drawn wagon.

"Well, now, it be two miles or maybe more out Crookedwood Road," said the man.

Greg assumed he was thinking in "Old Irish" miles, which meant that the distance was probably closer to one mile.

"Would yer lady like a jar o' sweetbreads?" the man asked. "Or how about a bit o' home-cured bacon?"

"Oh, let's have the sweetbreads," said Greg, pulling money from his pocket. "And please tell me where to find Crookedwood Road."

"Why, through Crookedwood Forest, of course," said the Irishman with a big smile. "Would she enjoy some cruibins now?" he asked, pronouncing it "croobeans."

"Sure, why not." Greg handed over the additional money, knowing this game could damn well go on all day if he kept playing. "The Crookedwood Forest," he repeated. "Where is it? Exactly?" He made a face that let the Irishman know the game was over.

"Sure n' yer standin' in it," the man said, grinning. "This be Crookedwood Road!" He pointed to his right.

Greg couldn't help laughing. He'd been the butt of a "fine joke."

"What was that all about?" Robin asked as he climbed back into the driver's seat. He handed her the two jars. "Sweetbreads?" she asked.

"Animal glands."

"Greg! And what's this other one? Crui—I can't pronounce it."

"You'll like it a lot. It's pickled pig's feet."

Robin giggled. "You actually paid for this stuff?"

"No. I paid for directions to Reilly Castle. You got the 'stuff' free."

~~~

Crookedwood Road was everything the name implied, a crooked road— actually a narrow, paved lane—through crooked woods. After just a mile, as Greg had suspected, the woods thinned to a lovely meadow. There were a few farmhouses; then, the little castle came into view on the left, sitting well back from the road. The wrought-iron gate was open. Greg turned the car onto the crushed-pebble driveway and drove slowly up to the stone home. The stillness in the car was palpable.

"Are you all right, Robin?" he asked.

She was very quiet. She only nodded, staring at the two crenellated towers on either side of the enormous wooden door. Matted ivy crept up the tower walls.

"Robin?" Greg stopped the car and touched her arm. "Is it *déjà vu*?" he asked.

"No," she whispered. "It's the real thing. Oh, Greg, I've been here before. I'm sure I have!"

Very slowly she climbed out of the car and walked toward the steps. Above the door was a wooden sign with an Irish blessing that read, "God spare you and those you meet until your journey is done." Beside it was a green shamrock, indicating Bord Fáilte (Irish Tourist Board) membership.

Robin stepped aside, allowing Greg access to the huge brass doorknocker; then, she turned, taking a few steps to the right, where wildflowers of every color of the rainbow had bunched themselves into a garden.

Greg smiled at the tall, gentle-looking woman who opened the door. "*Dia's Muire dhuit,*" the woman said.

Fortunately, from his other visits to the country, Greg knew the proper response. "God and Mary and Patrick be with you," he replied, referring, of course, to the Holy Mother and the Blessed Saint.

Just then Robin turned back to face Gilda Lynch.

And Gilda Lynch fainted.

CHAPTER 10

Greg caught her just before she hit the cold, hard stoop.

"Here, now! What's this?" Hurrying across the gravel from the left was a short, stocky, weathered-looking man with tufts of red-gray hair poking from beneath his cap.

"Help us! She's fainted!" Robin cried. But Greg had already lifted the woman as if she were a feather.

"This way, this way," said the man, moving in front of them. He pushed the big door inward and directed them straight ahead, across the polished stone floor of a cavernous entry room to a huge central fireplace, where four Victorian loveseats were arranged around the hearth. A low fire burned in the grate, but it wasn't exactly cozy. Robin had a brief impression of being in a church. A narrow stone staircase circled up the right side of the room.

Greg lay Gilda Lynch on one of the small sofas and pulled a patchwork quilt across her legs.

"You must be Fergus Halloran," Robin said to the man. She was startled to hear her voice bounce off the walls.

"That's right, Miss." He looked up at Robin then…and quickly crossed himself. "Holy Mother of God!" Removing his cap, he backed up and sat directly on the hearth, landing with a thump. Speechless, he was.

"She's coming around," Greg said, tending his patient.

"Well, we're about to lose another one." Robin pointed toward Fergus, who remained gape-mouthed on the hearth, staring at her.

"It's the lass!" cried Gilda Lynch, pushing herself up with her hands. "It's the lassie come home!"

A line out of TV reruns! Robin didn't know whether to laugh or cry. She felt like the central character in a very bad comedy. By this time the housekeeper was sitting up straight, making room for Greg beside her, and Fergus had closed his mouth.

"Lass?" the woman asked shyly, searching Robin's face.

Robin pulled up a footstool to sit on. "Mrs. Lynch—"

"No missus, lass, just Gilda. Please."

"Gilda...do you know me?"

. The woman smiled. "Whatever ye call yerself, ye be Robin Reilly for sure. There'll be no mistakin' that!"

Tears sprung up in Robin's eyes, and the scene was no longer funny. Someone in Ireland knew who she was.

"Oh, Robin darlin', don't cry. It's ever so glad to see you I am." Gilda reached forward and touched Robin's dark shining hair just briefly. "So many years," she said. "So many years."

"How...how many?" Robin gripped the sides of the footstool.

"I don't even need to think about that one," Gilda said, smiling. "Ye be thirty-five years old now, so it's been thirty-four years ago last month since I saw ye."

"And you...you recognized me after all that time?"

"But of course!"

Fergus Halloran made a choking noise. "Fergus," Gilda said. "Why don't ye bring us all some tea. You know where the pot is. And let's move to the drawing room. This big space is only good for evening prayers, where God and all His angels can hear the words as they bounce off the walls and into heaven itself. And that's reminding me, it is, that there'll be plenty to thank Jesus and the Holy Mother for tonight!" She started to rise then faltered and sat down again. "Fergus," she said, "better bring me a sip o' claret along with that tea. I'm feeling a bit weak."

She rose once again, this time with Greg's help, and directed them to the drawing room, which was on the right, beyond the stairway. It may have been a small room for a castle, but it was still bigger than Robin's entire loft! Or maybe the high ceiling just made it seem that way. Here the fireplace was small but extremely ornate, with some fine pieces of old Irish crystal on the mantle. A painting of an aristocratic young gentleman hung above. Robin searched the face for a resemblance to herself or to Patrick but found none.

"That's Mr. Ronan Reilly in his youth, God rest his soul," Gilda said. "Here's a more recent picture." She lifted a framed black-and-white snapshot from a marble-topped side table and handed it to Robin. "This was taken just before his last sickness. Eighty-two years old, he was."

Robin was stunned to see a man looking no more than sixty-five, a nice-looking man with light eyes and fair hair, or maybe it was gray. He seemed ageless, unmarked by time. "What did he do to stay so young?" Robin asked. "Did he work?"

"Ronan Reilly didn't 'do' anything. He was rich, and then he wasn't."

Fergus came in with a tea tray and set it on the low table in front of the fireplace.

"Fergus," Greg said. "Would you mind showing me the grounds? I believe these ladies have a lot to talk about."

"Sure 'n we'd be better out of it!" Fergus replied, with a pixie grin. They left through a door in the back wall.

Gilda offered Robin a wing chair, which Robin found surprisingly comfortable, and took the one opposite for herself.

"I'm sorry about Mr. Patrick's passing," Gilda said. "That Mr. O'Súileabháin told me." She pronounced Sullivan in the old way. "But he didn't tell me you'd be coming; though, it's glad I am that you did!" She paused and looked over her shoulder. "I like your young man. Are ye married, lass?"

"No. Oh, I'm sorry! I didn't introduce you. He is my very dear friend, Greg Haviland. I live on his grandmother's hunting plantation in Florida."

"Ahhh," Gilda replied as if that explained everything. Expertly, she poured tea, adding a drop of claret to her own cup.

"Gilda, please tell me about when I was here before. I don't remember anything, not any of it. When we pulled up out front, I knew I had been here. I didn't remember the castle, really. It was just a feeling. Was I born here?"

"Oh, you poor wee lamb! And that's what you were then, too, a poor wee lamb not as high as my thigh when ye came." She tucked a strand of gray hair back under its pins. "No, darlin', you were born north, in Ulster, and came here in late October of 1969, just a few months after I took up employment here."

"October? But that's only two months before I arrived in the United States!"

"That's right. Only two months you were here 'n they whisked you away. Cried me heart out, I did, but o' course I had no say in the matter. Mr. Patrick Reilly was heading for America to find his fortune as if there really was a fortune to be found at the end of the rainbow, and there was nothing for it but that ye go with him and Anna. It was bad then, but Eire's fortune has changed, lass. There's a future here now for the young people."

Robin could see that keeping Gilda Lynch on the subject might be a problem.

"Gilda, who is Wren Reilly?"

Gilda nearly spilled her tea. "Ye don't know? No, of course not. Mr. Ronan Reilly was a one for keepin' the bits o' his life all nice and neat, in little boxes, so to speak. He was sure you could have a grand life in America, but only if ye were cut clean away from yer beginnings. Life was not good in Northern Ireland in 1969, and life was especially not good in the Reilly family then. Ah, lass, it's been a hard thing, a very hard thing." She shook her head with a sigh.

"Who is Wren Reilly?"

"For the life o' me I don't know why ye were never told. But Mr. Reilly thought it was for the best, and when Mr. Reilly decided something, it stayed decided." She put her teacup on the table and stood. "Come, lass. It's time ye met Wrenny."

~~~

When Greg saw how beautiful the castle grounds were, not immaculately groomed but pure wild grandeur, he returned to the car for his camera then followed Fergus Halloran toward the back of the property.

"No formal gardens anymore," Fergus said. "'Tis all I can do to keep it cut back." He pointed to the left, where some bright flowers grew around very old statuary, chipped and broken. "That little patch I keep as clean as I can with the time I've got because Gilda insists. Ye can see it used to be real fancy. Fact o' the matter is there've been no formal gardens here for goin' on forty years, but that was before my time. In the old days, homes like this had a staff o' gardeners with nothing to do but garden. Imagine that! Me, I got me own place to take care of besides this one. Now what would ye be wantin' a picture o' *that* fer?"

Greg was aiming his camera at a garden of flowers gone wild. There was certainly no dearth of material here! The more wild it was, the better he liked it. "I think it's attractive, Fergus," he replied.

"Aren't you a one, though. Most folks want grounds to look like a host o' little people had cut each blade o' grass with finger scissors!"

Greg laughed. He had taken several good shots of the castle, too. His grandmother would enjoy them. Fergus had told him that there were eighteen rooms, which was certainly small compared to the thirty-eight rooms at Haviland Plantation, but Reilly Castle's rooms, with their high ceilings, seemed cavernous. Twelve bedrooms, he had said, but only five were open; three were for paying guests. Mr. Reilly's room, of course, was closed.

According to Fergus, one good thing had come of that—they didn't have to listen to the "blathering television" any more.

"That was all the old man wanted in his last days," Fergus said. "Television all day long 'til bedtime! *News* programs, one after 'tother, as if we needed news in Ballylith. Years before, it was just morning *and* night he played the thing."

They were walking through the woods now, and Greg knew that he would come back again by himself for some really good nature photos. He ached to roam the entire estate with his camera.

"Do ye want to see the family cemetery? It's just beyond the wee hill."

"By all means," Greg replied. He was enjoying himself thoroughly. At first he had felt guilty, leaving Robin on her own, but something told him it was best that way.

Fergus apologized for the condition of the cemetery and at the same time relieved himself of blame because, after all, it hadn't been used for years until Mr. Reilly's burial. "Strange, that. Himself not wanting a wake," Fergus said. "All Irish love a good wake. Sometimes a wake lasts all the night with clay pipes and snuff provided for everyone."

"Snuff?"

"Sure 'n the box is placed on the chest of the deceased, an' when we each go up to get our pinch, we check for signs of life. Makin' certain, we do."

Greg suppressed a smile, saying nothing.

"But then, Mr. Reilly was a strange man," Fergus continued. "He didn't like the keening, for one thing, and he didn't have any friends for another. 'Tis true though, he told Gilda and me when would be the exact day of his death, and it was! He had that gift. And he was able to keep the life in him 'til the priest came. Mr. Reilly was quite a man, he was."

Weeds and moss crept over the gravestones, each of which, Greg noticed as he moved the brush, contained a line or two of eulogy, often humorous. The letters were black with age. "What are the plaques for?" he asked, pointing to his right.

Fergus removed his cap and put it across his heart. "Those are for all the souls over the years whose bodies, for one reason or another, could not be returned from the fighting for proper burial. God help us, sometimes our cemeteries have more plaques than gravestones."

~~~

Gilda Lynch had led Robin to the back of the castle and down a corridor where inadequate wall sconces served as the only light. Faded squares along the walls were evidence that paintings had once hung there. Gilda caught Robin's glance and explained, apologetically, "They had to be sold. Most of them were old masters, too. But it takes a lot o' money to keep up a place like this."

Robin was glad to see bright sunlight coming from a window at the end of the corridor and from the doorway of a room on the right. As they neared the room, she heard music. Lovely music!

Gilda had a broad smile on her face. "Do you like the sound o' the harp?"

"It's beautiful!"

"'Tis a miracle, that's what it is. She plays like an angel."

They stepped into the room, and there in the corner, bent over a tall golden harp, was a young woman with dark coppery hair just like Robin's. Robin held her breath so as not to disturb her. The music was delicate with a flowing melody expertly played with passion and an obvious love of the instrument. When the song was finished, Gilda guided Robin toward the harpist, saying, "Wrenny, darlin', someone's come to visit."

Wren Reilly stood then and turned to face Robin. Her skin was what some folks call "peaches and cream;" her eyes were a clear green, and her smile was bright. And Robin Reilly felt she was staring at her own image in a mirror. She gripped Gilda's arm for support.

"Wrenny," she whispered as agonizing memories of the terrible parting suddenly washed over her. *The Robin and the Wren. Twins!* Tears of anguish rolled quietly down her face, but still she could not move.

Wrenny lifted her hand and touched Robin's cheek. "A mirror is it? But there's no glass." She seemed bewildered.

"Not a mirror, darlin'. 'Tis Robin come home!"

"Robin?" The lovely smile grew, and the eyes sparkled with joy.

Gilda turned to Robin. "Wrenny's an 'innocent,' lass. Reach out to her."

"An innocent?" Robin didn't understand.

"Her mind didn't grow like yours did. But her heart is full o' love, and she's been waitin' for you for thirty-four years."

"Robin?" Wrenny repeated.

With a heart-wrenching sob, Robin Reilly gathered her sister into her arms.

Wrenny

CHAPTER 11

"Wrenny, darlin'," said Gilda, "why don't you play a song especially for Robin?"

"Would you like that?" Wrenny asked, her eyes wide with delight. "I would like to play for you!" Robin, still overcome, could only smile and nod.

Wrenny began with a little tune that Robin had never heard, and then she started to sing as she played:

I wish I had the shepherd's lamb,
the shepherd's lamb, the shepherd's lamb;
I wish I had the shepherd's lamb, and Katie coming after.

She sang the chorus in Gaelic, but it didn't matter that Robin could not understand the words. Wrenny's voice was sweet and clear and entirely natural, and Robin thought it was the loveliest sound she had ever heard. There were several verses, many of which, Gilda said, Wrenny had made up herself, all followed by the Gaelic chorus. Then, suddenly, she started playing something Robin knew, "Londonderry Air." The tune, played with Wrenny's sincerity and tenderness, started Robin's tears flowing all over again.

"Ye know," Gilda said, "that the great composer, Handel, once said he wished he had written that song."

"I have never been more touched by anything," Robin whispered.

"Ah, the *gultrai*—music to make us weep," Gilda said. "If anyone's to weep over Londonderry, 'tis the Reillys. But Wrenny also plays *geantrai*— music to make us laugh!"

Wrenny stood suddenly, abandoning the harp. "Oh, Robin! Would you like to see my room? I want to show you my room!" She grabbed Robin's hand and pulled her toward the corridor.

Robin looked over her shoulder to see Gilda's bright smile covering her whole face. "Enjoy yerselves!" Gilda called.

They moved quickly back down the corridor, the way Robin had come, and into the huge entry hall, reminiscent of medieval times. To the right of the imposing front door was a small mahogany door leading into the tower. Wrenny opened it and went ahead of Robin, up the winding, stone stairway—the second such stairway Robin had seen in the castle. The steps had been worn smooth by four hundred years of scuffing feet, and Robin was very glad that a safety railing had been installed in later years.

At the top, a door opened into a lovely, bright room that could only belong to a child. Pictures and mobiles hung from a wood strip around the walls and stuffed animals were everywhere. The flooring was a fairly new parquet with a big, soft, furry rug to make it cozy. And, of course, the inevitable fireplace was there to make it warm. Sunlight streamed in through latticed windows from three angles.

"Do you like it?" Wrenny asked, flopping onto the four-poster.

"Very much! I like it very much, Wrenny," Robin answered. She could not help noticing the bars on the windows, but she was glad they were there.

"You talk funny. Why is it you talk funny?"

Robin sat beside her on the bed. "I guess it's because I've lived most of my life in another country. People pronounce their words a little differently there." Robin's soft Southern accent was showing.

Wrenny smiled. "I like the way you sound. Say something else."

"All right." She thought a moment. "How's this? 'Look to the rainbow; follow it over the hill and the stream. Look, look, look to the rainbow; follow the fellow who follows a dream.'"

Wrenny clapped her hands. "It's a rhyme! It's a rhyme! I make music with rhymes."

"Yes, in fact, this rhyme already has a tune. It was written in my country, but it's about the rainbow in your country. *Your* rainbow."

"Oh, Robin, if you sing it to me, I can play it on my harp. I know I can!"

"I'm sure you can. We'll do that later."

"What else does the rhyme say?"

"Well, it says 'it's a rhyme for your lip and a song for your heart. Sing it whenever your world falls apart.'"

Wrenny laughed. "World falls apart! That's funny! The world won't fall apart!"

Oh, but it does, thought Robin. *Thank God you'll never know it.* "My father...*our* father," she said, "used to sing it to me when I was a little girl."

"My father is dead."

"Yes, I know."

Wrenny jumped up suddenly and lifted a rag doll from a rocking chair, hugging it close to her body. It was dirty and threadbare. Tufts of hair were missing, and its padding was lumpy from years of loving. After a tight squeeze, she turned it around. "This doll's name is Robin," she said, proudly. "Now I have *two* Robins!"

~~~~

That evening Robin, Greg, Wrenny, and Gilda had dinner in the pleasant dining room where paying guests were always served. The furniture was Regency and the table would seat eight at full capacity. Tonight, however, Robin and Greg were the only guests. Because it was a special occasion, Gilda had asked Peig Morgan to come from the village and cook a meal of boiled ham and cabbage: Wrenny's favorite.

Gilda had laughed good-naturedly when Robin handed her the jars of sweetbreads and cruibins earlier that afternoon. "I see ol' Cap'n Mackey caught you with his blarney!"

"He caught Greg, not me."

Gilda chuckled again.

After dinner, Robin went with Gilda to the scullery to help with the dishes while Wrenny and Greg played chess or, rather, played *at* chess. Gilda had told Greg that Wrenny knew how to move the pieces—that pawns move forward, bishops diagonally, and so forth—but that she had no grasp of strategy. Still, she loved to play in her own way, and she was delighted to have a new playmate. Fergus usually challenged her to a game each week.

"She's really happy now, that one," Gilda said, meaning Wrenny. But Gilda, herself, didn't look happy. She sighed. "What will ye be doing about her?" she asked.

"What do you mean?"

"Ah, lass, don't send her to that awful place Mr. Reilly picked out. She's slow and a little fey, but she's far from stupid. She doesn't belong in a place like that!"

Robin put a dish carefully in the cupboard. Everything had happened so quickly; the day had been so unreal that she hadn't thought beyond it. Of course she would have to do something about Wrenny!

"Gilda," she said, "what exactly were Mr. Reilly's plans for Wrenny, for you, and for the castle?"

"Y' mean ye haven't heard the will?"

"I'm afraid I didn't stay with Mr. O'Sullivan long enough to give him a chance. He told me that I would inherit most of the estate, but I'll have to go back to Tralee to settle things."

"Well," Gilda sighed again. "Mr. Reilly told me that you or Mr. Patrick could do with the castle what you would, and if neither of you came, I was to close it up forevermore. He left me the little farmhouse across the road, and oh, it's fixed up ever so nice! Did you see it when you drove by?"

Robin nodded though she really hadn't noticed the farmhouse so intent was she upon the castle. "And Wrenny?" she prodded.

"Hmmph. He made arrangements for her to go to one o' those *homes*." She spat it out as if it were a dirty word.

"You mean a home for the mentally ill?"

"That's it, an' a cryin' shame it is! I wanted to keep her with me, like me own she is. I've raised her from a lamb, but he said no, she'd either be livin' like a Reilly or be off to have 'proper' care. Poor Wrenny, she'd soon die of a broken heart, she would. Why, I'd take good care of her, allowance or no allowance. A member of the Legion of Mary, I am!"

Now it was Robin's turn to sigh. "Gilda, how is the castle doing financially?" she asked.

Gilda let the water out of the sink and dried her hands. "It's goin' under. That Mr. O'Súileabháin in Tralee sends the same wee monthly allowance that Mr. Reilly set up years ago with never a raise in it. There was no use talkin' to Mr. Reilly about the cost o' livin' going up because he wouldn't hear of it. When he got sick this last time, I had to start selling things to keep up. I know 'twas wrong of me, but there was no other way. There still isn't. That's why I wrote to Mr. Patrick and why I was lookin' for him to come. I was hopin' he could make sense of this fine kettle o' fish. I didn't know he'd be dyin', too, God rest his soul." She made the sign of the cross.

"What about the income from paying guests?"

"We have maybe six or eight guests a month, and though we charge 'em an arm and a leg, that's not nearly enough to pay the bills. Not many folks want to spend a night in Ballylith. Whyever should they? There's nothing here."

"Did you speak to Mr. O'Sullivan about it?"

"I did. He said there was nothing he could do because Mr. Reilly was sure-fire stubborn about the amount o' the house allowance, thinking that way the money would last at least until he died. It's possible Mr. O'Súileabháin could raise the allowance some, now that Mr. Reilly's gone, but it still won't last Wrenny's lifetime."

"How was Wrenny's, uh, 'home' to be paid for?"

"Oh, she has a separate trust fund from her parents, well, *your* parents, too, but we can't use it here except for a small amount that keeps her fed and clothed. I understand there a good bit o' money there, but it's meant only to take care o' Wrenny now and after there's no family left. Irish families take care o' their own, you know. Wrenny's trust is a *good* thing, it is. I find no fault in that, only in Mr. Reilly's decision to send her away."

"Where is this place, Gilda?"

"Up near Limerick." She sniffed. "Not even in County Kerry, for goodness sake! Ah, please, lass, I'm begging. Ye can do something about it, ye can. Ye'r *family*!"

Robin hung the dish towel on a wall peg, feeling more overwhelmed than ever. And angry, too—at Patrick, Anna, Ronan, and all the other Reillys, if there were any. Certainly she would take care of Wrenny. Emotionally, she had no choice. She was tied as tightly to her now as she would have been, had they never been separated. Oh, *why* had Patrick done this? More to the point, *how*? How could he possibly have afforded to set up a trust fund for Wrenny, when he was going to America to "seek his fortune?" More lies! Had he ever intended to tell Robin the truth?

She sat down, pulling up to the heavy wood-block table. "Gilda, tell me about the Reillys of Ballylith. Where have they gone? What happened to them?"

Gilda frowned as if this were irrelevant. "Why, Reillys have always lived at Reilly Castle, what few of them there were. They weren't known for their breeding, excuse me for saying. Mr. and Mrs. Ronan Reilly had no children."

"What about my grandparents? Did they live here, too? What were their names?" .

Gilda hesitated just a little. "I never knew them, y' see. They died young, long before I was grown."

It was difficult to tell how old Gilda was, but Robin guessed her to be in her late fifties, early sixties. "Their names?"

"Tomas and Kathleen, so I'm told."

Well, that was one thing Patrick hadn't lied about. He had told Robin their names. "Gilda, how did Wrenny and I come to be born in Ulster?"

This time Gilda held her breath as if deciding what to say, but "Don't know" was all she said. Then, "I think we'd better go fetch Wrenny. It's time for evening prayers." She was clearly finished answering questions.

Why is it, Robin thought, *that the Irish can go on with one sentence for a full minute without a breath and then close up like a Gulf Coast clam the very next second?* She recalled a bit of Patrick's wisdom: "We hear only what we want to hear, and say only what we want to say."

· Once more they went into the big entry room, which Gilda referred to as "the Hall." This was where Gilda and Wrenny, and sometimes Fergus, met each evening for prayers. Two boxy, ornate medieval guild chairs stood against one wall, and fade marks beside them indicated that two others had been sold. Above was a leather wall hanging, hand-painted in a flower motif. There was a large picture of the Holy Family above the fireplace, and a candle lantern hung suspended from the ceiling.

Gilda began lighting the candles, giving the place an eerie glow. It looked and felt like an illuminated cave with just about as much warmth. Robin wasn't at all sure she liked it, and she was absolutely sure Greg wouldn't like it, coming from a dyed-in-the-wool Southern Methodist family. Nevertheless, he came and sat politely on one of the loveseats, observing but not taking part. To Robin's amazement, Wrenny, with some prompting from Gilda, was able to lead the rosary. Then Gilda followed with the after-prayers. It was early when they finished, just nine o'clock, but Wrenny was accustomed to retiring at that hour. She gave everyone a hug and went up to her tower room, saying it was the most wonderful day of her life.

Gilda, too, was ready to retire. Robin's and Greg's luggage had been taken to their rooms earlier by Fergus, who'd set it down in front of the wardrobes. The castle had no closets. Robin's room was directly above the music room and across the hall from Greg's. Even though these were guest rooms, Robin noticed the threadbare carpet and faded draperies and the lack of paintings or vases or throw pillows—anything that might have lent a special touch. If Gilda were "charging an arm and a leg," as she claimed, she probably didn't have repeat visitors.

"Let's go for a walk," Robin said to Greg when they were finally alone. Greg would have liked to take her around the grounds, as Fergus had taken him, but the lack of outside lighting—it cost too much to keep it up, Fergus had explained—made a tour impossible at night, especially this night. No moon, no stars. They stopped at the car for a flashlight, then started down the gravel drive toward the road to Ballylith. Their heavy, wool sweaters and jeans felt good in the cold night air.

At first they didn't talk, both occupied with thoughts of their own. Greg's feelings about this day of revelation were mixed. He remembered Patrick, in his drunken stupor, babbling about a castle in Ballylith, and he remembered thinking that if there were Reillys at a castle in such a place, they couldn't be any better than Patrick. Now there was Wrenny, a precious gem if ever there were one. And Ronan. *He may be dead,* Greg thought, *but his presence certainly lingers in every room of that musty old cavern.* As far as Greg was concerned, Ronan Reilly had been the devil incarnate, despite O'Sullivan's claim that he wasn't a "mean man." He could think of no good reason for separating a pair of twins and keeping that information from them. What was it he had written? Something about the "coming of age." Pure bunk. And why hadn't Patrick had more backbone? Why hadn't he taken both girls with him? Why did he abandon Wrenny? It simply wasn't the Patrick Reilly Greg had known. As far as he was concerned, there were still pieces missing from Robin's puzzle. *Big* pieces.

"What are you thinking about?" Robin asked, slipping her arm through his as they turned onto the road.

"Just trying to make sense out of a day that makes no sense at all."

"I know. I've been over it again and again in my mind, and I still don't understand. I'm emotionally exhausted." She sighed. "I believe that today I went through the highest high and the lowest low of my entire life. And the questions! There are so many questions I'd like answered, yet I don't know where to turn. Wrenny can't answer them, and Gilda...I don't know about Gilda. I'm sure she knows more than she's telling."

"If so, she'll talk eventually. The Irish are consummate talkers, in case you hadn't noticed."

"Hey, I'm Irish," she said, smiling into the black night.

"Oops."

"There's one thing Gilda said that's been bothering me. Wrenny was playing 'Londonderry Air' on her harp, and Gilda called it by some Gaelic name and said, 'Music to make us weep.' Then she said, 'If anyone's to weep over Londonderry, 'tis the Reillys.' But right away she looked as if she shouldn't have said it, and she changed the subject. What's she afraid of? Ronan's dead. He's certainly not going to reach back from his grave and throttle her!"

"Let's start with your questions," Greg said. "Tell me what you would like to know, and we'll figure out, logically, where to find the answers."

"All right." She thought a moment. "I guess I'd like to start with my grandparents, Tomas and Kathleen. At least their names were the same, coming from both Patrick and Gilda. It's about the only common ground I've found though Gilda said she never knew them. Maybe if I can find out what happened to them, I can figure out why Patrick did what he did. I just can't understand why he separated Wrenny and me, and why he left her in that mausoleum with a crotchety old man."

Greg smiled to himself in the darkness. "First of all," he said, "even though you and I don't see it that way, Reilly Castle is perceived as a lovely old country home in these parts, not a mausoleum, and it's my guess that Ronan Reilly was not a crotchety old man at the time Wrenny was left with him. He must have developed a streak of eccentricity in later years to maintain that ridiculous secrecy, but I'm sure Patrick felt he had left Wrenny in good hands. Remember, too, that Ronan's wife, Maeve, was living at that time. When did she die, by the way?"

Robin had only to close her eyes to see every word of the letters she had found in Patrick's bedroom. "April of 1980," she replied. "Wrenny would have been twelve years old then."

"So Wrenny would have had a mother of sorts—or maybe Maeve was more like a grandmother—for about ten years. Maeve was obviously a good influence. Wrenny's a remarkable person." Robin thought that over. "But about your grandparents," he continued. "When Fergus took me around the grounds today, he showed me a family cemetery. It's overgrown with weeds and brambles, but I'll bet we could find their graves."

"Oh, let's! First thing tomorrow morning!"

"After that, why don't we visit the church in Ballylith? Surely there'll be some kind of roll book we can check."

"What a wonderful idea!" In her excitement, she tugged on his arm, causing him to drop the flashlight. "Greg," she said, paying no attention to the rolling beam of light, "I'm so glad you came with me." She reached up to give him a hug and ended in his strong embrace, her head resting on his chest.

He held her for several seconds, no longer surprised at his own stirred feelings. He was thinking not only of her beautiful body and the mysteries it held, but of the person—Robin, woman of contrasts. Fiery, kind, exciting, vulnerable. And the mysteries of her body became even more enticing.

Suddenly, she pushed away. "Greg! The flashlight's gone out! Where is it?"

"Should be fun finding it. This isn't exactly a moonlit night." It was black as pitch. Together on the ground, they groped for the flashlight, dirt caking their hands, and pebbles poking their knees.

"We'll never find it!" Robin blindly groped again, this time her hand clutching Greg's neck.

"That's not the flashlight," he said, playfully pulling her off balance. She fell on top of him as he sprawled out on the dirt road. One second later they were laughing and rolling into the ditch.

"Do you realize where we are?" Robin asked, her lips close to his.

"A very nice place," he replied, covering her mouth with his.

"Greg, we're on a *public* road! Someone may come by." She pushed him away and sat up. "And how are we going to find our way home? At this point, I don't even know which direction we came from!"

"Why don't we use the flashlight?" he asked, turning it on.

"You have it? Greg, you beast! And what a nice beast you are," she added, falling on him again, tantalizing him with tiny kisses. She surprised him with her aggressiveness, running her hands through his hair, nibbling his ears, nuzzling his neck.

Greg loved it. *I can last as long as you can*, he thought. He held her lightly, enjoying her playful moves for several minutes.

Finally, she rose to her feet. "Let's go back," she said. "My hair is full of dirt."

~~~

Old Mrs. Haviland would have been secretly pleased, if only she had known that in Robin's room, high up in Reilly Castle, something "happened" that night.

CHAPTER 12

Early the next morning, before Gilda or Wrenny stirred, Greg and Robin poked about in the old cemetery. The yellow gorse, still blooming, smelled like sweet coconut as they pushed it away from the gravestones to read the epitaphs. Some were simple statements about the person's life; some were humorous remarks; some didn't make much sense. The Irish, it seemed, had a great capacity for producing cheer in the midst of sorrow.

"Sure wish I had a gun," Robin said, kicking a dead branch aside with her booted foot.

"Why?"

"Why do you think? I told you I have an aversion to snakes!"

Greg laughed. "Relax, Robin. There are no snakes in Ireland."

She made a face at him and kept kicking her way along. "This place could use the talents of Jerome Davis and his landscaping crew."

"I'm serious," he said. "No snakes."

She stopped and studied his face. "You *are* serious!"

He nodded. "Saint Patrick chased them out."

She rolled her eyes.

"OK, so that's just a legend."

"Blarney, you mean."

"Nice blarney, though. But it's true there aren't any snakes in Ireland. It has to do with ice covering the whole island millions of years ago. When the glacial ice was finally gone, the land remained frozen for several hundred more years, and by the time the freeze ended several thousand years ago, frigid ocean water lay between England and Ireland. There was no way for a snake to *get* to Ireland. Same thing happened to New Zealand. No snakes."

"You're just full of useful information," she said, grinning.

"I'm a wildlife photographer. Snakes interest me, as well as all other critters. To change the subject," he said, "come, look at this." He moved to one of the older gravestones and placed his hand on it. The birth date came first, 10 June 1799, then the death date, 10 June 1814. "Mary Reilly," he read.

"So good at stalking the pheasants, the birds quit feeding at Reilly Castle in fright of her!"

Robin smiled. "Now that's an ancestor I can identify with." Then her smile faded. "Died on her fifteenth birthday. So young. I wonder where she fits on the family tree." Her toe stubbed against a different kind of stone. "What are these?" she asked.

"Fergus said they're plaques in memory of those whose bodies could not be recovered from the fighting. Some of the ones I've seen go back a hundred years. The later stones are in that corner," he said, pointing to his left. They moved forward and quickly found Ronan's and Maeve's graves, untouched by weeds. Other than the names and dates, the double headstone only bore a carved Celtic cross. No epitaphs.

"It's true, you know."

"What?"

"About the snakes."

"Right." Robin shook her head and kept walking.

It took just a few moments looking through this section of the cemetery to locate Robin's grandparents. Kathleen and Tomas had died in 1952. They shared a gravestone and an epitaph, which said, simply, "They loved and lost."

"That certainly is depressing," Robin said. "What do you suppose it means?"

"Probably not a damned thing."

"What?"

"Robin, from the vendors at Shannon Airport to Kern O'Sullivan in Tralee, to the farmer on Crookedwood Road to Fergus Halloran, and yes, even to Gilda Lynch, about three-fourths of what we've heard has been pure Irish blarney. Why not put it on a gravestone?"

Robin grinned. "I'm thinkin' ye'r an unbeliever, Greg Haviland," she said.

"That doesn't mean I don't enjoy it," he replied, smiling.

They continued looking through the stones but found no graves newer than Tomas' and Kathleen's, except for Ronan's and Maeve's. That made sense. Patrick had been an only child.

They arrived back at the castle in time for a hearty breakfast of eggs and sausage, warm soda bread with orange marmalade, and hot tea.

After breakfast Robin.went with Wrenny to the music room to sing "Look to the Rainbow" as she had promised. Robin's singing voice wasn't clear and beautiful like Wrenny's, but she sang in tune and was able to teach Wrenny the first four lines of the song rather easily. She was amazed at how quickly Wrenny adapted the tune to her harp. Gilda sat in the corner, tears of joy in her eyes, watching and listening to the two of them.

Then, without warning, Wrenny abandoned the music and pulled Robin, running down the hall and out the back door, to see her garden. Luckily, Robin was getting used to Wrenny's short attention span. The "garden," sitting well away from the house, was actually the decaying remains of a very old formal garden. Several pieces of elegant but crumbling statuary still stood, and a few wildflowers bloomed. Fergus, or possibly Wrenny, had obviously cleaned the area, but as far as Robin could tell, it was mostly a garden of weeds.

"Isn't it beautiful?" Wrenny asked, twirling in the pathway. She leaned down to sniff carefully at some of the nettles, which Robin was sure had no scent at all, prickly things. Then, lovingly, Wrenny reached up to touch a statue at the point where its arm was missing. "This is Father," she said of the image, which was two hundred years old if it were a day. "He's dead. I don't have a statue of Mother. She's dead, too."

"Well," Robin offered, "maybe I could buy one in the village or in Tralee, and Fergus could put it in your garden. Would you like that?" Robin knew they'd have to settle for contemporary junk, but it might please Wrenny.

"Oh, yes! Would you? Would you, Robin?"

Robin said she would. They spent the rest of the morning together, flitting from one thing to another like butterflies, wherever Wrenny's whims led them, while Greg was occupied elsewhere on the grounds with his camera.

After a quick lunch of open-faced sandwiches and tea, Gilda excused herself, and Wrenny announced that she would take a nap.

"While you're resting," Robin said to her sister as they moved toward the Hall, "Greg and I will visit the village. We'd like to see Ballylith. Maybe we can find your statue there."

"Statue?" Wrenny was blank.

"Of Mother. To go with the other one in the garden, remember?"

"Oh, yes! Thank you, Robin," she said, giving her sister a big hug.

As they were getting into the car, Wrenny called down from the window of her tower room, "Robin! Be sure it has two arms. Mother has two arms!"

"What was that about?" Greg asked as he drove down the road.

"I don't know," Robin answered, truthfully. "I really don't know."

~~~

In her cozy home at Haviland Plantation, Cassie Davis lay comfortably in bed. Jerome was beside her, propped up with pillows. He was reading the latest James Patterson novel. Just two hours earlier they had been at the hospital, where Cassie had endured the pain and, to her, humiliation of false labor.

"Jerome," Cassie said.

"Hmmm?"

"This is Tuesday."

"Umhmmm."

"Day after tomorrow is Thursday."

"Umhmmm."

"Jerome, put the book down for a minute. Please."

"Oh, sorry, honey." Reluctantly, he lay the book aside. "I was just at a good part."

Cassie smiled. "You're always at a good part. Did you know this is Tuesday?"

"So?"

"Thursday is Thanksgiving."

"So?"

"Jerome! What are we going to *do*?"

Jerome put an arm around his wife and said, good-naturedly, "I know what you're thinking. Big dinner, all the preparations, and now you don't feel like it. Well, it's no big deal. Miss Emily's going off with friends for the day. So there's just the two of us and your mom. Why don't I take you both out?"

"Out? For *Thanksgiving* dinner?"

"What's wrong with that?"

"It's not traditional."

"You sound like Miss Emily. Lots of folks go out for Thanksgiving dinner. Look here." He lifted the evening paper from the nightstand and opened it. "Here are ads from three different restaurants in Tallahassee— 'Come spend Thanksgiving with us.'"

"Jerome."

"Not another word. We're going out. Strawberry Alice will love it!" He chuckled. "You know she will. And the rest of the day we'll do what we're supposed to do—give thanks." He slid down beside her and kissed her nose. "For Berry, for you, and for that healthy baby girl inside of you."

"And for you, Jerome Davis," she said, kissing him back. "I love you!"

"Have you decided on a name?"

"Well, since Robin's my best friend, I thought a bird name would be nice."

"Sure. Warbler? Owl? Bald Eagle?"

"No, you silly thing!" Cassie punched him playfully. "I was thinking of…Oriole."

"Oriole Davis," Jerome said, trying it out. "Not bad. Not bad at all." He kissed her again, this time gently on the lips.

"Let's snuggle," she said.

"Umhmm, if that's the best we can do."

"It is. Say goodnight to James."

"Goodnight, James." Jerome tossed the James Patterson book onto the floor and turned out the light.

~~~

In Ballylith, Robin and Greg went straight to St. Mary's Catholic Church at the end of the main street, appropriately named "Church Street." It was a lovely, wooden building with exposed beams and straight-backed pews. The Stations of the Cross were carved from fine wood, and the lighting was soft and friendly. Robin felt comfortable as soon as they stepped inside. Fortunately, the priest was there, but unfortunately, he was young, new to the area, and not very helpful. He did, however, allow Robin and Greg to browse through the roll books from 1900 to the present. There were very few Reillys.

"Guess Gilda was right," Robin said. "The Reillys weren't good 'breeders.'"

Greg chuckled.

They found Ronan Reilly's birth in 1908 and that of his younger brother, Tomas, in 1912. In 1933 Ronan married Maeve Moriarty, and in 1935 Tomas married Kathleen O'Shea.

Robin stretched. Her shoulders ached and her eyes were tired from trying to read the spidery old writing on yellowed paper.

Greg stood behind her and massaged her shoulders. "Shall we quit for a while?"

"No, I want to finish. Patrick and Anna must be here somewhere. Maybe even Wrenny and I are in here."

"And maybe not. Remember, you were born in Ulster."

"Still, it seems to me that all of the family should be listed here."

They started reading again, and, eventually located one more Reilly—Sean Reilly, born to Tomas and Kathleen in 1944.

Robin stared, incredulous. "But Patrick said he was an only child! Sean would have been his brother. Do you suppose Sean died in infancy? Oh, Greg, keep looking!"

They searched on through to the present. Ronan Reilly's death was recorded on October 9 past; someone named Beatrice Wyse on October 15; and a baby, Michael McDonough, was born on October 29.

There was no mention of Sean Reilly after his birth. No marriage; no death. Robin double-checked. She then scanned back up the pages to 1937, where Patrick's birth should have been recorded. But there was no record of Patrick Brannigan Reilly, Robin's father. *Not anywhere.*

CHAPTER 13

"I know of one more place we can check while we're in the village," Greg said. "When Fergus and I were walking yesterday, he told me of an old gardener who had worked for the Reilly family for more than fifty years until his poor health got the best of him. He's ninety-four years old now and confined to his home, but Fergus said he enjoys having visitors."

Robin nodded. "Let's find him." She was still stunned over the discovery that Patrick was not in the church records.

After asking a few questions in the village, they found Liam O'Byrne in a cluttered, overheated room of a small farmhouse on the outskirts of Ballylith. He sat in a wheelchair, wrapped in blankets before a peat fire, and puffed on a foul-smelling pipe. And he was truly overjoyed when his daughter—a chunky, tired-looking woman in her seventies—introduced his visitors.

"Scones, Bridget," he croaked. "Hot tea and scones." He turned to his visitors. "One needs a good, hot cup o' tea in this drafty barn of a place."

In fact, Robin and Greg had already removed their sweaters; the room was stifling.

"It's very nice of you to see us, Mr. O'Byrne," Robin said as they were seated. "Especially without notice."

"Well now, what would I be needing notice for? In case I'd be going hurling?" He laughed at his own wit, and Bridget excused herself with a "humph" to prepare scones and tea.

"So ye be a Reilly, eh?" Liam O'Byrne was addressing Robin, a little too loudly. "And what branch o' the Reillys would that be? From down in County Cork, maybe? Or over in Limerick? I hear there's a bunch o' shirt-tails in Limerick."

"N-no," Robin answered slowly. "I believe my ancestors came from right here in County Kerry."

"Oh, do ye now." He puffed a billow of smoke from his pipe. "That's interesting."

"I'm Patrick Reilly's daughter."

"Patrick Reilly?" The old man gave not a flicker of recognition. "No Patrick Reilly in these parts. Must be the Cork Reillys ye're thinkin' of."

"Mr. O'Byrne," Greg said, "I believe you worked for many years at Reilly Castle here in Ballylith."

"Yep, I did."

"Were you there in the nineteen-thirties?"

"Well now, 'course I was. I took care—*good* care, mind you—o' the grounds at Reilly Castle from the time I was a young lad o' barely twelve years. 'Twas a good job, too. Respected me work, they did. Bridget tells me young Ronan died recently."

Young Ronan? Well, perhaps to Mr. O'Byrne a seventy-nine-year-old would seem young, Robin thought, smiling to herself. "That's right," she said. "He was buried last month in the family cemetery."

"Cemetery!" O'Byrne choked on smoke. "Last time I visited, 'twas, let me see…goin' on ten years ago, the cemetery was covered up with nettles and knee-high weeds, and the gorse runnin' wild, it was." He pointed at his guests with the stem of his pipe. "I'm tellin' you, me and my helpers would'a never let that happen. Kept it clear and clean, we did." He sighed. "But I guess they's only one gardener there now, and him not really a gardener a'tall, but a handyman? What can ye expect?"

"Mr. O'Byrne," Robin started, gently, "did any Reillys other than Ronan and Maeve live at the castle during the years you worked there?"

"Well, now, o' course. Ronan's daddy hired me, Mr. Seamus Reilly, and his mother was living then, invalid though she was." He thought for a moment. "Can't seem to remember her given name. Young Ronan took over when the folks died, and then his little brother, Tomas, brought his bride home to live, too."

"Were there any children?"

"Well, now." He liked to start his sentences with *well now*, Robin noticed. She also noticed that he considered this question very carefully. "Oh, Bridget, the scones. Thank you; that's a good girl." He paused while warm scones with currants and hot tea were served. As soon as Bridget had excused herself and disappeared, Liam O'Byrne leaned toward Robin and whispered loudly, "Bridget 'ud talk yer leg off if ye'd let her, but she's a good girl—knows when to make herself scarce. Just talks twaddle, she does." He settled back, dropping crumbs onto his blanket. "Now where was I?"

"The children," Greg prompted.

"Well, now. There was only one child. That was Tomas's Sean. Just a nipper o' six or seven he was when Tomas and his bride were killed in that godawful carriage accident, may they rest in peace. Bloody damn, that tea's hot!" he exclaimed, spitting it out. "Jesus, Mary, and Joseph!"

Robin handed him a napkin.

"Much rather have me pint o' Smithwick's, I would, but Bridget says it's not good for me, much it matters at my age. Ye'd think she'd want me to be happy, ye would. Say, young fella," he leaned toward Greg, lowering his voice. "Think ye could come to visit again and bring me a pint?"

Greg joined the conspiracy. "Do you suppose we could keep Bridget from finding out?"

"Damn sure be fun tryin'!" the old man cackled.

"We'll come back," Greg promised.

"Mr. O'Byrne." Robin had to try one more time, though she could see the old man was getting very tired. "What happened to Sean?"

"Sean?"

"The nipper?"

"Ah, yes. Well, now, he packed up and ran off when he was barely out o' his teens, he did. Never heard o' him again."

"He never came back?"

"Nope."

Greg rose. "Thank you, Mr. O'Byrne, for talking with us." He helped Robin to her feet. "We'll be going now."

"But ye'll come back?"

Robin smiled and patted his hand. "You can count on it."

"And ye'll bring the pint?"

"You can count on that, too!" Greg said.

~~~

"Uh-oh," Robin said as they drove through the gate on the grounds of Reilly Castle.

"What?"

"We forgot Wrenny's statue."

"She's probably forgotten it, too. We'll get it next time we're out."

They found Gilda Lynch in a nervous dither. Peig Morgan was cooking and baking in the kitchen, and Fergus Halloran was polishing silver and complaining about it.

"Women's work! They've got me doing women's work!" he cried.

"It's not women's work, Fergus," Peig returned with good humor. "It's work, period, and that's what you're paid to do, so do it."

"Sure 'n a woman's tongue never rusts!" he replied.

"Guests have arrived," Gilda explained, wringing her hands, "for *two* nights. *Paying* guests. They didn't have reservations, but I couldn't turn them away. I just couldn't!" She added in a whisper, "We need the money."

"Of course you couldn't turn them away," Robin said. "We'll help. Tell us what to do."

"It's not that. It's…well, there's two couples and we only have one spare room now, what with you and your young man here. I took the liberty o' movin' ye'r things up to Wrenny's room, Robin, if y' don't mind sharing for a couple o' days."

"I don't mind at all," Robin said. "That's a perfect solution, so relax and let us help you." There was no time to dwell on Patrick's name not being on the church roll, nor remembered by Liam O'Byrne.

"Oh, bless you, darlin', for being so understanding. These guests are real nice, and they look ever so rich!"

Greg volunteered to help Fergus with the silver, which mollified Fergus somewhat, and Robin was assigned the task of dressing the dining room table—fine Irish linen, china, Waterford crystal and a centerpiece, which she was to create herself from rhododendron leaves and wildflowers.

"Would ye be hostess tonight, Robin?" Gilda asked, before they resumed working.

"Hostess?"

"'Twould be a treat to have the real owner of the castle as hostess."

Robin gulped. Did she really *own* this monstrosity? "How do you usually manage the dinners?" she asked.

Gilda blushed, guilt-stricken. "Well," she replied, slowly, "in order to make it the most fun for the guests, I've been dressing meself up kind o' grand in Mrs. Reilly's clothes, God rest her soul, and playing Lady o' the Manor, God forgive me." She crossed herself.

Robin smiled. "I see no reason to change things, Gilda. To tell you the truth, I wouldn't know how to be a 'grand lady.' Maybe I can learn from you. Are Greg and I invited to dinner, too?"

"Oh, but of course! That'll make us just eight, a full table. Bless you, child!"

~~~

The dinner was great fun. Everyone dressed up, and Gilda put on a "rare show," upping the power of her Irish lilt to grand form. Of course, she'd had years of practice, watching Maeve Reilly. Even Wrenny was skilled in elegant manners, though she remained quiet the whole time, no doubt on Gilda's instruction, for Gilda made a big point of telling the guests how *shy* Wrenny was. *More blarney*, Robin thought. Wrenny had vacant moments and a short attention span, but she was a most outgoing, loving, and delightful person. Not at all shy! Still, Robin did the talking when the guests commented on how identical the twins were, and how beautiful. Wrenny would smile and dip her head coyly. Greg just tried to keep from laughing. He said later that he couldn't remember when he'd had so much fun at a dinner table.

After dinner Wrenny enchanted everyone with her harp in the music room, even performing one couple's request, "The Rose of Tralee." Gilda had said on the first day that Wrenny's music was a miracle, and Robin was sure now that it was.

Evening prayers in the Hall were not "done" when guests were in residence, lest there be Protestants in the group, and God forbid the Reillys should offend anyone. But Robin and Wrenny said theirs privately, high up in Wrenny's tower.

~~~

Greg lay awake a long time. He was getting so caught up in the life of the Reillys that he hadn't thought about photography the entire day. To him, that was incredible. Now, he thought about last night and about the wonder of being with Robin in bed, about the tenderness of their lovemaking, and about how much he wanted her in his arms this minute. He smiled, wryly, into the darkened room. If only Gilda had moved Robin into *his* room instead of into Wrenny's.

Bunratty Castle

CHAPTER 14

Robin was up early the next morning to help Peig in the kitchen. The guests were to be served a very special breakfast in bed—a kedgeree of boiled rice and salmon tossed in hot butter, then mixed with chopped hard-boiled eggs. With it would be a pitcher of fruit juice and barmbrack with hot tea or coffee if the guests preferred. Robin was slicing the barmbrack, a wonderful-smelling bread, thick with cinnamon, raisins, and currants. As they worked, they talked.

"How long have you been cooking here, Peig?" Robin asked.

"Oh, just since herself passed away. Guess that's been twelve years or so now. Before that, I'd come out sometimes t' help her, if there were too many guests or if she wanted to serve something she didn't know how to cook, like some o' those fancy dishes she found in magazines. She was a one for magazines! And him with his television." Peig smiled fondly. She was an attractive, matronly woman with graying black hair and lively eyes. "I remember the two of us slaving over some concoction of pork, prunes, and pastry. It sounds awful, but, believe it or not, it was delicious, and the guests thought they were tasting some ancient royal recipe!"

"You liked Maeve Reilly, didn't you?"

"Oh, my, yes! She was a one! Had a real sense of humor, she did. I cried my eyes out when she died. Heart, it was, took her real sudden."

"Did you know my grandparents, Tomas and Kathleen?"

"No, dear. They was before my time."

"Did you know their son, Sean?"

She shook her head. "He was gone before my time, too."

"Peig, did Maeve ever tell you what happened to Sean?"

Again, Peig shook her head, a little more slowly this time. "No, dear. She would never talk about Sean, and I hadn't the heart to ask her. The talk in the village is that he up and left one day and was never heard from again, though everyone thinks there's more to it than that, seein' as how Mr. and Mrs. Reilly loved him like he was their own son, rather than nephew. They say it was a tight little threesome. Then, one day it was as if young Sean never existed. Ye'll find no snapshots of him around here. Unless they're in that locked room upstairs that used to be his bedroom, that is. No one ever goes in there. 'Course you could now, seein' as how you own the place."

"Maybe sometime," Robin said. "Did you ever hear of Patrick Reilly, my father?"

Peig thought a moment. "Well, there was a Patrick Reilly came to visit a couple o' times, maybe forty years ago. I suppose 'twas the same one."

Robin nearly dropped her knife.

Peig smiled shyly. "The reason I remember was, I met him on the road to the village, and I thought he was the handsomest fellow I'd ever seen, and Irish from his head to his toes! He introduced himself and smiled a big smile and carried on like I was some kind of queen though I wasn't even ten years old at the time. I was in awe of him, I tell you, because I had never met a young Reilly before. But when I asked him about the castle, he said he was just a visitor. 'Just a humble visitor,' he said, doffing his hat and dipping his chin like a popinjay. Humble, my foot!" She laughed. "He was full o' the blarney."

So someone besides Gilda had met Patrick. Maybe there were others. If he were merely a visitor, as he had claimed, then he wasn't necessarily a "castle" Reilly, which would explain why his name wasn't in St. Mary's roll book. But then, that would mean that Wrenny and I aren't "castle" Reillys either. So why should I inherit?

"Did Patrick say where he came from, Peig?"

"Ulster. Belfast in Ulster, he said."

"You said 'a couple of times.' When did he return to Reilly Castle?"

"Well, maybe more often, but the only time I know of was a few years later, when he and his wife came—don't think I ever heard her name—then turned right around and took off for America. That's what I heard. I didn't see him then."

Anna, Robin thought. *His wife's name was Anna. And no one ever mentions her. Were her beginnings too humble for the Reillys? Had she no dowry? Or was she overlooked because she was quiet and shy?*

Just then Fergus Halloran appeared at the back door.

"A little later than usual, aren't you, Fergus?" Peig asked. "What makes you think there's any breakfast left?"

Fergus removed his cap and turned on his best pixie grin. "Now, Peig me girl, I know you saved me something good, some rashers and eggs, maybe?"

"Rashers and eggs! Not for these guests, it's not. We're making a kedgeree fit for royalty."

"Ah, c'mon, Peig, a man can't go hunting on a twiddly breakfast like that!"

"Hunting?" Robin's ears perked up. "What are you hunting, Fergus?"

"Pheasant. Peig here's goin' to use up the last o' the pheasant in the freezer for tonight's dinner. Can't be without pheasant in the freezer."

Robin held out a piece of barmbrack. "May I go with you, Fergus, please?"

Fergus snatched the barmbrack and bit into it. "You? A slip of a lass? And raised in a foreign country at that?" He shook his head. "Too dangerous."

"I'll make you some rashers and eggs! What's rashers?" she quickly asked of Peig.

Peig laughed. "It's lean bacon. What he wants is warming in the oven, but we won't give it to him, will we, unless he takes you hunting."

Fergus hesitated then pulled out a chair and sat down. "Women! Y' can't trust 'em, no way. I'll have me breakfast now."

"And Robin will be going with you?" Peig asked, her hand on the oven door.

He shrugged. "Can't say I'm over the moon about it." He enjoyed a long, dramatic pause then said, "Sure 'n why not? But ye'll have to do what I say, mind ye, and stay out o' trouble." He pointed his finger at her for emphasis.

Robin ran to him and gave him a big hug. "Thanks, Fergus! I'll get ready and be right back. Enjoy your breakfast!"

He smiled and shook his head as she ran from the room. "That one's going to lead some young fellow a merry chase!"

"I'd say she's doing that already," Peig replied, thinking of Greg Haviland. Couldn't help noticing the way he looked at Robin.

~~~

Greg, too, had risen early. He had taken his camera and tramped the environs of Ballylith until nearly noon, not scouting for anything in particular, just capturing on film a host of beautiful scenes and interesting moments. Sheep and goats were not exactly "wildlife," but they did provide him with some good shots. And then there were the walls—Ireland's low stone walls everywhere, going nowhere, enclosing nothing. A lovely mystery. All considered, the morning had been productive and satisfying.

~~~

Gilda was in the kitchen, getting a glass of water when Robin and Fergus burst through the back door. Robin was laughing, and Fergus was fussing, his Irish accent so thick it was nearly incomprehensible.

"Why dinna ye tell me ye cud shoot li' tha'?" he was saying. "Here I wuz a-worryin' meself half to death o'er a poor wee lass who dinna deserve me worry!" He turned to Gilda. "Would ye believe this lass hit ev'r pheasant she aimed at and most o' the ones I aimed at, too?"

Gilda covered her mouth with her hands and laughed 'til she shook.

"Here, now!"

Robin put their quarry in the sink. "Think of it this way, Fergus, we got twice what you would have brought back on your own. And didn't you enjoy yourself? Come on, now, admit it!"

Fergus folded his arms across his stocky little body. "I still say a woman's place is in the home!"

Wrong thing to say to Robin Reilly. "And I say that's nonsense! It's probably something you heard on television!"

"I don't listen to the blatherin' television!" he cried.

Just then Greg came through the door. "What in the world is all the fuss about?"

But Fergus wasn't finished with Robin. "You've a bit of a temper there and no mistake," he said, shaking his stubby finger at her.

"You mind yer tongue, Fergus Halloran. Yer speakin' t' the queen o' the castle now." She nodded pointedly toward Robin.

Fergus took a big breath, readying a reply, then changed his mind and snapped his mouth shut, shaping it into his now familiar pixie grin.

"My goodness, what a fine lot o' pheasant!" Gilda said, peering into the sink. "Fergus, you really are a marvel!"

"Now wait. She—" Fergus started, but Robin cut him off with a finger to her lips.

"He was terrific," Robin said. "We don't have pheasants where I come from, and he was kind enough to let me tag along. I had a great time."

"Next time, Fergus, *I* want to go with you to see the pheasants." Greg said. "Just to take pictures," he added, pointing to his camera, "no guns."

Fergus softened, the grin forming again on his face. "Sure 'n why not," he said. "It might be kind o' fun."

The four of them settled around the kitchen table for a lunch of cold ham and salad. Wrenny had gone to the village with Peig Morgan, and the guests would be out until dinner time doing "touristy things," Gilda had said. "And wouldn't the two of you like to do something touristy, too?" she asked. "Ye haven't seen anything of our beautiful Eire since ye been here, except Ballylith, and God knows there's nothing much here. I'd be thankin' the Holy Mother for that, 'cept we could use a little something to attract guests. Not too many folks want what's quaint an' quiet."

"There is something I'd like to do," Greg said. "When we drove down from Shannon, I told Robin that I'd take her to dinner at Bunratty Castle." He turned to Robin. "What about tonight? If we're lucky, maybe they can squeeze us in."

"My, now!" Gilda exclaimed. "That'll cost ye many a pound, ye'll see. Now that's what I call takin' in *payin'* guests!"

"Robin, would you like to go?"

She hesitated only briefly. "I'd love it if Gilda doesn't need us here."

"Lass, I've been managing this place on me own for twelve years now, since herself passed over, and I can manage it one more night." She looked at Greg. "Ye'll have to be stayin' there the night, though. That's a distance, it is. There's plenty o' good bed-and-breakfast inns nearby."

Greg excused himself to make the calls.

"My! Bunratty Castle!" Gilda said. "I hope he'll think to reserve two rooms, lass. It wouldn't do to stay in one, even with twin beds."

Robin glanced at Fergus, who rolled his eyes heavenward.

~~~

So they traveled to Bunratty Castle.

To Robin, whose only experience with castles was the tiny, molding, Reilly Castle, Bunratty was magnificent. Where Reilly Castle was no more than a country home made of stone, Bunratty was a gigantic medieval fortress, restored to its former glory. Like Reilly Castle, it had a central, vaulted "Hall," though much larger and on the second floor. From the Hall, Robin and Greg were able to see stone stairways to the wine cellar, the chapel, and the huge banqueting room below, where they would have their evening meal.

They arrived in plenty of time to climb a circular stairway up one of the turrets to the keep and to look out over the Ratty River at a considerable portion of Counties Clare and Limerick, an unforgettable view! But the best was yet to come.

Soft lighting in the banqueting room came from candles, as in former days. They were met by Irish serving maids in fifteenth-century costume, who presented them with the traditional "bread of friendship." They were then "bibbed" and seated at a long table presided over by an honorary Earl, and beakers of honey mead were provided all around.

"This is good," Robin said, taking her first sip.

"Watch out—it's more potent than it seems."

"Well, I'm sure when the 'hearty meal' is served, the potency will be diluted." She took another sip.

In just a few minutes dinner was served—pork chops, several vegetables, and uncut loaves of bread. The servers then transformed themselves into entertainers, singing and playing harp and fiddle.

Robin looked at the food in front of her. It was steaming hot and looked and smelled delicious. She whispered to Greg, who was seated beside her, "Where's the silverware?"

"Beside your plate."

"I only have a knife."

"My dear," Greg replied, "we are now in medieval times. A knife is all anyone gets. Look around the room."

Sure enough—everyone had a knife. Only a knife.

"...for *peas*?"

~~~

"Gee, it's a pity you forgot to reserve two rooms," Robin teased as she lay contented in Greg's arms. After such a heady, other-worldly evening, they had made love quickly, impatiently and passionately, like fifteenth-century lovers on the run.

"Actually I asked for two rooms, but there was only one left."

She turned to peer at him in the darkness. "You didn't."

"Right. I didn't," he said, covering her mouth with his.

They made love again in the big soft bed, this time slowly and sweetly. And this time Robin was aware of much more than physical passion. Greg was truly *loving* her—gently touching the magical places, kissing, caressing with his mouth and with his eyes, anticipating her responses of pleasure, then giving more, and more, and more...and, finally, all of himself. Suddenly her pleasure crested and waves of purest joy surged throughout her body. She clung to him, tightly, holding him within her. And in that moment Robin Reilly realized that she had fallen in love with her childhood friend. The knowledge shocked and scared her. This was no longer a mere "lovely time" with a very good friend. It was real. And her body began to tremble because she suspected he felt the same. Why hadn't she seen it coming? Her mind began to whirl. She was excited and at the same time depressed, for they would both be in for a lot of misery. There'd be no future for such an incompatible pair! Catholic-Protestant, hunter-photographer, tempestuous-gentle, poor-rich....

"What are you thinking?" Greg whispered close to her ear.

She turned her head so she could look at him, then took a deep breath and replied wryly, "I'm thinking that I live over your *garage*, Greg."

"Ah, but you own a *castle*," he said, kissing her nose.

Robin giggled. "Some castle—riddled with debt and decay! When is your birthday?" she asked suddenly, propping herself up on her elbows.

"July twenty-fourth."

"Oh, great." She flopped back onto the pillow. "You're Leo, and I'm Capricorn."

"So what?"

"The Lion and the Mountain Goat. They don't mix."

He grinned and cupped his hand under her breast. "I thought we were mixing pretty well."

"That's not what I meant," she replied, removing his hand.

"What did you mean?"

"Astrologically speaking, you and I are incompatible."

"That's a crock."

Very tenderly she kissed him and said goodnight. *We should have taken Gilda's advice,* she thought as she turned away from him, burying her face in the pillow. *We're too different. Should have booked separate rooms. Because nothing will ever be the same again.*

She lay awake most of the night.

CHAPTER 15

The morning was misty and fresh, and the uneasy lovers spent part of it ambling around a re-creation of a nineteenth-century Irish village on the grounds of Bunratty Castle. They bought several postcards. It took two cards for Robin to write everything she wanted to tell Cassie Davis. Greg wrote his grandmother and promised her an "evening of photos" when they returned to the plantation.

They decided to take a different road home, this time through Listowel, where they had a stew-and-sandwich lunch in a pub, washing down the sandwiches with big mugs of dark brown Guiness stout. In one corner a group of old men sat nursing their pints, and off in another corner some young people sang Irish songs, many of which Robin had learned from Patrick during her childhood.

As she sat listening and tapping her feet to the rhythm of "Molly Malone," she thought life just couldn't get much better—a lovely drive, an incredible banquet, the awakening of love (no matter how elusive), and now these beautiful memories of Patrick and his music. She smiled. Was that Patrick she heard whistling? It was almost possible to forget her troubles. Almost.

On the outskirts of Listowel, Robin noticed a shop sitting well back from the road. It had garden equipment, plants and statuary clustered—or rather, "cluttered"—around the entrance.

"Stop here, Greg, please! Maybe we can find Wrenny's statue!"

"Tell me again what she wants," he said as they got out of the car.

"She calls her statue—the one with the broken arm—Father, and she says that she doesn't have one of Mother. She wants a female statue."

"With two arms."

"Right." Robin rolled her eyes.

They stepped over pile after pile of pure trash before Robin finally spotted her treasure. "Look, Greg, a pair! Adam and Eve. Wrenny can place them together somewhere in her garden and forget about the broken statue. I just hope they aren't too heavy."

The statues were fairly light, made inexpensively of hollow plaster, but the design was good. They could be weighted down with rocks on the inside. Robin was pleased. With careful packing, one fit into the trunk—or the "boot," as the salesperson said—of the car and the other into the back seat.

~~~

As they approached Reilly Castle, they met Peig Morgan bicycling toward them on the drive.

"Hello there!" Peig called, stopping beside the car. "I stayed a wee bit longer to help Gilda clean up. The guests have checked out; the sheets are clean, and everything's back to normal, I hope. Did y' have a good time?"

"A wonderful time!" Robin said. "Is Fergus here? We found some statues for Wrenny's garden."

Just then Wrenny came running down the drive, a look of relief and exasperation on her innocent face. "Robin," she called, "I missed you! Oh, Robin, you went away! Why did you go away?" Her beautiful green eyes were filled with tears. "I thought you wouldn't come back!"

"We told her you'd be back," Peig said to Robin, "but when you were gone the night, she wouldn't believe us."

Robin got out of the car and gave Wrenny a big hug. "Of course I'd come back, Wrenny dear. You shouldn't have worried."

"You're my *real* Robin." Wrenny cried against her sister's shoulder. "Don't leave me, Robin! Please don't leave me forever." And Robin knew then that she never would.

"Wrenny," Robin said, "we brought you a surprise."

"You asked about Fergus," Peig quickly injected. "He has the rest of the week off."

"Surprise? What surprise?" Like a child, Wrenny's mood changed instantly to one of bright expectation.

"It's something for your garden," Greg said. "And since Fergus isn't here, I'll help you with it. Come get in the car and we'll drive out back as close as we can get."

"Take my seat, Wrenny," Robin offered. "I'll walk."

As Greg and Wrenny drove slowly away, Peig straddled her bicycle once again. "Robin," she said, "I've thought of someone who might be helpful to answer some of the questions yer asking. I don't know the answers, and Gilda won't talk. Don't blame her for it. She's loyal 'even unto death,' as the Holy Scripture says. But Kate Keegan might help. She's very sensible."

"Kate Keegan?"

"She was Maeve Reilly's best friend. Perhaps her only friend."

~~~

Greg lifted the big packages from the car and placed them in an old wheelbarrow that Wrenny found for him.

"Over here!" she called. "This is where Mother goes." She was standing beside the broken-arm statue.

"Wrenny, let's take the wrappings off so you can see what we have. I think you'll want to choose a different place for them."

She unwrapped the female first. "Oh, she's lovely, she is! This is Mother, pretty Mother! Now I have a mother!" Greg helped her unwrap the male. "Who's this?" she asked. "He's very handsome."

"This is a new Father statue. See, they're a pair. They belong together."

"That's not Father!" she said, adamantly. "That one has two arms."

"That's right. You won't need the broken statue any more," Greg said. "You can put the new ones together in a different place."

Wrenny looked puzzled. "I don't think I can do that," she replied slowly. "Why not?"

"Because Father had only one arm. Gilda said so. She said he lost an arm."

~~~

Kate Keegan was a retired schoolteacher who lived in a modest, well-kept house on Mallow Street in Ballylith. Robin had telephoned, and Mrs. Keegan had graciously agreed to see her. She greeted Robin with a smile, a pot of tea, and a plate of warm gingerbread.

"My goodness, but you look like Wrenny!" she exclaimed as they sat side by side on the comfortable sofa. "How I wish Maeve was here to see you. She never stopped wondering about you, what had become of you. Oh, she knew you were fine with Patrick and Anna, but she had no news about little things—your schooling, your hobbies, things like that."

"Patrick and Anna...you knew Patrick and Anna?"

"Only through Maeve's conversation. I never met them."

"If she had just asked about me as I was growing up...Patrick would have told her. Wouldn't he?"

"She wouldn't have asked. Just hoped she might hear."

"Why didn't the Reillys of Ireland and the Reillys of America communicate? Why didn't they?"

"Oh, my dear, it's a very complex situation, and even I don't know all of it. Maeve confided in me to a certain point, but beyond that she kept things to herself. She said it was a matter of honor."

"Why were Wrenny and I separated?"

"Now *that* I can tell you. After you'd been at the castle just two months, it was clear to everyone that you were smart as a little fox. Going to America with Patrick and Anna made good sense. You'd have the advantages that you could never be given in Ballylith, especially at impoverished Reilly Castle."

"But why were we cut off from the rest of the family?"

"They felt it was best for Wrenny. She would never be able to understand or accept a separation, and old-fashioned as it may seem, Ronan also felt that Wrenny's obvious condition might be a drawback to your progress if you remained together."

A drawback! Robin thought. *My beautiful sister? What a cruel, old-world way of handling things!* She swallowed hard, a pinpoint of awareness growing from deep inside her. She wasn't sure she could handle the answer to her next question, but she had to ask. She just *had* to. "Was Wrenny...born like she is?"

Mrs. Keegan replied as kindly as she could. "No, dear. Wrenny was injured in a bombing in Ulster."

Robin's eyes filled with tears. *The dream. The horrible recurring nightmare!* That was how it had happened. Wrenny had been hit by something flying through the air, and Robin had come out of it unscathed. Until that terrible moment when the bomb exploded, scattering its devastation with fiery terror, Wrenny Reilly had been just like her sister—a normal little girl, one who laughed and played and asked thousands of questions. *She never had a chance. Not one chance!* Robin stifled a sob, then broke down completely and wept, her head on Kate Keegan's lap.

As her crying subsided, she sat up and wiped her eyes with a napkin from the tea table. "I'm sorry," she said.

"Don't ever be sorry for feelings."

"Mrs. Keegan, why were we there? Why were we there in the middle of the fighting at all? Surely we could have left the area earlier." Robin's frustration was mounting. "Why weren't we here in Ballylith? At Reilly Castle?"

Kate Keegan sighed. "Before you were born, Robin, your father chased a rainbow. What it was, I don't know, but unfortunately, it was something entirely unacceptable to his Uncle Ronan and Aunt Maeve Reilly, and for that matter, it would have been unacceptable to everyone in Ballylith had it become public knowledge, according to Maeve. And I must accept that because Maeve was an intelligent woman."

"But Patrick was always chasing dreams. Some of them may have been far-fetched, but they were harmless. He was a *wonderful* person!"

Mrs. Keegan hesitated briefly, then said, "Let me hold your hand, dear."

Robin gave her hand to the lady and felt the gentle pressure.

"Patrick Reilly was truly a wonderful man," Mrs. Keegan said. "Don't you ever forget that. But he was not your father. You and Wrenny are Sean's children."

CHAPTER 16

Robin held her tongue and her temper throughout the evening meal in the castle kitchen. Greg, Wrenny, and Gilda were devouring elegant leftovers, but Robin could only pick at her food. She was angry with Gilda for not telling her, for making her ferret it out on her own, but she hadn't yet confronted her. She hadn't even had an opportunity to tell Greg, and it was taking an enormous effort to keep quiet in front of Wrenny. Robin kept reminding herself that Gilda had been born with the Irish sense of high honor, and though she was kind, generous, witty and charming, she would honor her late employer's requests without feeling the least guilty.

"Have ye never eaten pheasant, Robin? Sure 'n it couldn't taste so different from yer quail, now could it?"

"It's fine, Gilda," she replied. "I'm just not hungry."

"Too much o' that fancy food up the road, I'm guessing. Well now, eat ye a little o' my bottled fruit. It's refreshing." Robin obliged with a spoonful of raspberries.

"Oh, Robin, I love the statue of Mother!" Wrenny exclaimed for about the one-hundredth time. She had placed the male statue in another part of the garden, then ignored it completely. "Mother" now stood beside "Father" with the missing arm, and Robin knew why. Kate Keegan had told her that Sean's arm was blown off in the fighting. Somehow Gilda must have slipped the information to Wrenny, unintentionally, of course. Perhaps when Wrenny had shown an interest in the broken statue, Gilda had said it resembled her father, who also had a missing arm. Wrenny might have found comfort in that. She certainly had found pleasure in her bond with the broken statue.

"I'm glad you like it, Wrenny," Robin replied.

After the meal Wrenny and Greg went to the drawing room for a game of chess, giving Robin the opportunity to speak to Gilda as they cleaned up the kitchen.

"Gilda," Robin began, "I went to see Kate Keegan today."

"Oh?" The sudden tension was almost palpable.

"She told me something that you wouldn't. Or couldn't."

"Couldn't."

"I know now that Sean Reilly was my father. Mine and Wrenny's." Gilda remained stone-faced. "But I don't know why his having children has been kept secret."

Gilda's nose went up in the air. "At least Kate Keegan has a *few* scruples." She sniffed.

"Kate didn't know. Gilda, are scruples really important at this point?"

"For certain they are!"

"Why? Have you considered what all of this secrecy has done to me? And to Wrenny?" Her voice rose. "Can you imagine what it's like to find out that the man you've known and loved as your father for thirty-five years isn't your father at all?"

"Thirty-three."

"Gilda!" Robin's patience was about gone, and her temper was getting the best of her.

"You don't understand," Gilda replied, looking a bit wild-eyed herself.

"You're right! I don't understand! But I want to. And you're not helping one bit!"

"I can't, child," Gilda replied with less vigor. "I just can't...I promised." She returned to her dishes, burying her arms to the elbows in soap.

"I'm going to find out, Gilda Lynch, even without your help! I'm going to find out *who* I am, and why I am *what* I am, and why I was packed off to the United States, and *with whom*."

"Ah, lass." Gilda sighed as she let the water out of the sink. "Ah, lass," she repeated. "Let's sit at the table a minute."

Robin hung her towel on the wall peg and sat down, Gilda across from her.

"I knew ye'd come some day," Gilda said. "But it was all supposed to be handled nice 'n legal 'n proper by that Mr. O'Súileabháin in Tralee. Well, if his grandfather was alive, things would've been different, but young folks these days don't feel the sense of responsibility that the old do. Ye were never supposed to see Wrenny, lass. She was t' have gone t' the home before you arrived. If only y' hadn't seen her, ye'd be on yer way back to America all content now."

"Content! Didn't you think I'd want to know my own sister? My *twin*? I've been having nightmares about her for years!"

"Ah, but the pain of knowing her as she is."

"Gilda, this is pain I can deal with. I *love* her." Robin took a deep breath. "There is no way to express to you how glad I am that young Mr. O'Sullivan shirked his high and mighty duties, making it possible for me to learn the truth, and I'm thinking he deserves a *gift*, he does!"

Gilda smiled. "Ye're beginning to sound like one of us, lass."

"I *am* one of you!" Tears of frustration welled in Robin's eyes. "Why am I not accepted?"

"Oh, darlin', you are accepted. Mr. Reilly left everything to you, didn't he now?"

"Everything except what really matters," Robin replied. She took another deep breath. "Who were Patrick and Anna Reilly?"

"Distant cousins. Lived in Belfast and visited here a few times. Part o' Northern Ireland's persecuted Catholics, they was, and when Mr. Reilly heard they were on their way to America for a better life, he sent for them and asked if they would take you. Well, it turns out they were childless and unable to have one of their own, so it was no wonder they fell in love with you on sight. They really did love you, Robin."

"I know that. They were my parents in the best sense. But why didn't they take Wrenny, too?"

"Oh, they tried, believe me, they tried. You should've heard that Anna, a little slip of a thing, arguing with Mr. Reilly, but he wouldn't give in. He said because Wrenny was an innocent she belonged here in her own country, where folk would love her and accept her just as she is. They do, too, you know. Folk in Eire treat the innocents with great compassion."

"She would have had a good life with us, too," Robin said, her eyes again filling with tears. "We lived on a beautiful plantation with acres and acres of land, and horses and dogs, and a lake with ducks…and some of the most wonderful people in the world. I would have loved growing up with her." She paused to blink back tears. "Why didn't Patrick tell me about her?"

"Because Mr. Reilly told him, if he did, you would be disinherited. Personally, I believe that Mr. Patrick looked around here—the place was much nicer then—and figured you'd be a wealthy woman one day, and he didn't want to ruin things for you, especially since he was unsure of his own future, what he could do for you an' all."

Robin shook her head. She felt as if it were full of cobwebs. It was amazing, the differences in what people found important. As if she cared about a musty old castle! "Gilda," she asked. "What was my mother's name? Sean's wife?"

But Gilda Lynch was finished talking. She compressed her lips and stared at the floor.

Robin quickly stood. "I won't be attending evening prayers tonight. I don't feel much like praying!" When she reached the door, she turned. "Tomorrow I will be going to Belfast!"

Young Robin has courage, thought Gilda. *She'll have what she wants out of life...if her temper doesn't get in the way of common sense.*

~~~

Late that night Robin sat next to Greg in the very masculine sitting area of his bedroom. Actually, Robin thought it was gloomy—mounted birds and animals on cold stone walls, lampshades of colored glass casting eerie shadows—but there was a fire in the grate and a lovely patchwork quilt tucked around her legs and, best of all, Greg's arm around her shoulders.

"All Kate could really tell me," she was saying, "was that Sean went to Northern Ireland—actually to the Queen's University Belfast as a student—and never came back. She said he was involved in the fighting and had lost an arm. Oh, Greg, he wasn't even as old as I am right now!"

"Did he bring you and Wrenny to the castle?"

"No. Kate said we arrived by courier; first me, then Wrenny a couple of months later. By the time Wrenny arrived, Patrick and Anna had taken me to America."

"Could your parents still be alive?"

"Kate didn't know, but she said she didn't think so because she felt that Sean would have come for us. She said he had 'too much inside' to forget about his daughters. She couldn't speak for his wife because she never saw her. It was someone he'd met at Queen's. Kate didn't even know her name because Maeve said it must never be spoken. She was telling the truth, Greg."

"Did she say why he never came back?"

Robin nodded. "Sort of. She said Ronan and Maeve disowned him. Maeve never told her why, but she seemed uncomfortable about it. Kate figured it was Ronan's decision, and Maeve went along with it reluctantly. They were very upset when Sean chose Queen's, and they refused to finance his education. They wanted him to stay in the Republic to go to University College Dublin. Then, after he'd been gone awhile, all communication stopped. I wonder if my mother might still be alive. Or her parents, my maternal grandparents. And how do I find them without a name? I'm sure Gilda knows, little good it does me. She'll never say it."

"So we'll leave for Belfast first thing in the morning. It will take us the better part of the day to get there."

"And there's so little time left," Robin said. "I have to be back at work in Tallahassee in ten days."

Greg squeezed her shoulder. "You'll be there," he said, "and by then, you'll know all you want to know about your family. We'll dig it out." His voice was assuring. "Now let's tuck you in bed," he said, giving her a hand up. "We'll both need a good night's rest."

He wrapped the patchwork around her shoulders for the walk across the cold, drafty hall. At her door he looked into her troubled eyes then pulled her body tightly against his own, kissing her hungrily, as if he couldn't get enough. He wanted very much to tell her he loved her, but he delayed too long, and the moment passed. *Better to wait, anyway*, he thought. *Wait until all this Reilly business is put to rest.*

~~~

They started a little later than they had intended because Robin wanted to explain to Wrenny, personally, that they would be back in a few days. She didn't want ever again to see the desolation in Wrenny's eyes that was evident the last time Robin had been away. She wanted to be sure Wrenny understood that Robin was her sister for keeps.

As they finished packing the car, Gilda appeared with a peace offering— a picnic basket filled with wedges of beefsteak-and-kidney pie, hard-boiled eggs, fresh fruit, slices of barmbrack, and two Thermos bottles of hot consommé laced with sherry.

"Ye'll be needing this, I'm sure," she said, handing the basket to Greg.

"Thank you, Gilda," he said. "It looks great."

"Robin," Gilda said, "I'm, uh...I'm sorry ye have to make this trip to Belfast. I must say I'm a little worried, especially after the recent goin's on up there in the Ardoyne District. Seems there's no end to the violence."

"What happened?"

"Bunch o' demonstrators threatened Catholic children with foul words and a pipe bomb, and all they were doing was walking through a Protestant area on their way to school. Threatened the *children*, mind ye!"

"We'll be fine," Greg offered.

"Still 'n all, I'm kind of glad ye'r going. I'm thinking maybe everything needs to be cleared up before any of us can rest in peace, most of all, you,

Robin, and Wrenny." Robin did not respond. "And I want you to know," Gilda continued, "that I don't know as much as you think I do. Honestly. I ·really don't know ye'r mother's name. It was never spoken in this house."

"Thank you, Gilda," Robin said.

Just then Wrenny came flying out of the house with her rag doll. "Robin!" she cried. "Oh, Robin, take her with you! When she's with me, she's Robin, but when she's with you, she can be Wrenny. See, Robin? You'll have me with you! I wish I could really go with you," she added quietly.

Robin thought her heart would break. She hugged Wrenny and thanked her for loaning the doll. "When we get back," she said, "Greg and I will take you someplace special for a day. If you can't decide where you'd like to go, we'll choose together. That's a promise."

"Oh! Could I see the ocean? Or ride on a bus?"

Robin laughed. "We'll talk about it in a few days. Meanwhile," she said as she held up the doll, "I'll have *this* Wrenny to remind me."

~~~

They took the N7 from Limerick to Dublin; then, they took N1 up the east coast to Dundalk. Luckily, Greg had the foresight at the time they'd rented the car to ask for the necessary papers to cross the border. Just north of Dublin they found a nice picnic area to spread out the lunch Gilda had packed, and as Robin hungrily devoured the food, she found that her attitude toward Gilda Lynch had mellowed somewhat. Gilda may have been close-mouthed and stubborn and firmly entrenched in her ways, but she also was a caring person with a strong sense of family and responsibility. She had certainly proven that in her relationship with Wrenny, particularly in the years since Maeve Reilly's death.

There were very few cars on the road, compared to the crowded highways of the United States, and the speed limit was 55 mph all the way. Even so, with the hills and curves and the wonderful distraction of some of the most incredible scenery Robin had ever seen, it was 6:00 p.m. when they arrived at the customs checkpoint that would allow them to cross the border into Newry, Northern Ireland. The checks were quick and friendly, first by the Republic of Ireland, then by British Customs. Just north of Newry, the Royal Ulster Constabulary had set up another checkpoint for inspection of passports. Again it was quick and amiable.

As they approached Belfast, Greg looked toward Robin, who'd been unusually quiet. "Are you nervous?" he asked.

She nodded. "Yes. Yes, I am. I don't know what to expect. In a way, I'm frightened. I know that things are different up here, that there's a lot of violence, but I'm ashamed to say I don't really understand what it's about. I can't imagine, for example, arguing with you—not to mention *fighting*—over the fact that you're Protestant and I'm Catholic. You see? What little I know…makes no sense at all."

"Someone once told me that the best thing you can take to Northern Ireland is an open mind."

Robin smiled. "That does make sense."

They had booked into the Forum Hotel on Great Victoria Street, right in the center of the city, because it would provide easy access to all points of Belfast. In the gift shop Robin picked up brochures and a map of the city.

"Dinner?" Greg asked, after they were settled in their room.

"I couldn't eat a thing," Robin replied. "Gilda's lunch was more than enough, especially in mid-afternoon. Besides, I'm still uneasy. Restless. I've never been anywhere like this or done any kind of digging or searching. I've never *had* to." She stood close to him and slipped her arms around his neck. "I'm so glad you're here with me," she said.

Gently, he kissed her. Then, as her arms moved across his back and her lips parted, he deepened the kiss, fully tasting her sweetness. Effortlessly, he carried her to the bed and slowly, button by button, opened her dress, exposing the fine lace of her lingerie. He kissed the smooth, soft skin between her breasts, breathing in the delicate scent of her cologne. And there was no holding back. Robin cried out in pleasure as he loved her and loved her. And loved her.

Later, as they lay entwined in the dusky twilight of the quiet room, each was thinking of the other. Even though she knew she loved him, Robin was convinced that nothing could ever come of their relationship because they were too different.

Greg thought the same; nevertheless, Robin was the woman he loved. It was as simple as that. And as complicated.

He turned his face to hers. "Robin," he whispered.

"Yes?" she replied, brushing her lips against his.

"Oh, what the hell. I love you, Robin!" he cried.

CHAPTER 17

They began the morning with a big, wonderful breakfast, celebrating their newly expressed love. Such a feast would surely hold them until afternoon tea, allowing plenty of time for uninterrupted searching. Greg hoped he could keep his mind on Robin's past, rather than on her future. He had to remind himself that if this issue were not resolved, Robin Reilly would never be at peace. She had told him as much after declaring her love for him.

"You know who you are, Greg," she had said. "I have to know who I am before I take the next step. *You* have to know who I am."

"No, I don't."

"Yes, you do!" Her Irish temper had flared briefly before they'd made love again. But it was enough. Greg knew that they had to go on, to wherever the elusive Reillys led.

Breakfast was traditional Ulster—eggs, bacon, sausages, fried potato bread, black pudding, and fresh dulse. Greg passed up the pudding, and Robin politely declined the dulse when she learned it was seaweed.

This was Saturday, and for a change, it was not raining or even misting. The sun was out, not warm like the sun of North Florida but very pretty and most welcome. Robin hadn't expected Belfast to be such a busy metropolis. She didn't know what she had expected, certainly not an ancient, decrepit village, but here was a thriving city of more than four-hundred thousand people moving about in buses and taxis. There was very little private auto traffic. The Albert Clock Tower struck 9:00 a.m. as they boarded Number 59 bus to the Public Records Office on Balmoral Avenue.

"It's a place to start," Greg said. "They have all the registers of baptisms, marriages, and burials for Northern Ireland. We'll find Sean Reilly."

"But all we have is his name, and he wasn't born in Northern Ireland. Maybe he never established residency. And we don't know exactly when he was here or for how long." She sighed. "It seems so impossible!"

"Are you talking yourself out of this before we even get started?"

"No, of course not. I'm sorry."

But the Public Records Office was closed on Saturday. "Open 0930-1645 hrs., Mon.-Fri.," the sign said.

"Now what?"

"Now we go to the next best place," Greg said. "To the Queen's University. If he were a student there, as Kate Keegan said, they'll surely have information on him."

"Will they be open on Saturday?"

"Be optimistic," Greg replied, though he had his fingers crossed behind his back, old Southern custom.

Back on the bus, this time up Malone Road to the university. Robin was astounded, not only at the size but also at the beauty of the university complex. The main building, over a century old, was brick Tudor with mullioned windows, and the entire area was dotted with charming Victorian terraces and magnolia trees.

"Magnolia trees!" Robin exclaimed. "Just like in Florida!"

The campus was a bustling place—people everywhere, even on Saturday. And they were dressed much the same as Robin and Greg, in jeans, sneakers and windbreakers.

"You should have worn black sneakers," Greg said.

Robin looked down at his black-clad feet, then at her white ones. "Why?"

"Look around you."

She looked, seeing only a smattering of white shoes in a sea of dark ones. "So?"

"Only Americans wear white sneakers. You'll be spotted as a tourist right away," he answered with a smug smile on his face.

"And you think you won't?" she asked, grinning.

"Of course not."

"Well, look around you, Mr. Know-It-All. Look at the faces. They're European, like mine. I was born here, remember."

Greg slyly scrutinized each person, greeting them as he and Robin walked along hand-in-hand. "Hmmm. And what makes me so different?"

"Americans are mutts." She laughed at the look he gave her. "It's true. Europeans have a distinctive look; Americans don't."

"I'm a *mutt?*"

"A very nice one, I must say." She squeezed his hand a little tighter.

Just then they caught the attention of a passerby, a handsome young man in a Donegal tweed jacket and matching cap. "American, are you?" he asked, looking straight at Greg..

They both burst out laughing. "Yes! I'm Greg Haviland. And this is Robin Reilly."

"Reilly? Now that's an Irish name," the young man said. "Are you by chance tracing ancestors?"

"How did you know?"

His face lit up with a bright smile. "Lots o' folks do that, especially this time of year. They come to the festival and poke about in the records while they're here."

"Festival?"

"The Belfast Festival here at Queen's. You mean you're not here for the festival?"

Robin shook her head. "We didn't know about it."

"Well, now, it's just the biggest arts festival in the United Kingdom—drama, ballet, music, whatever you like—though it's winding down now. This is the last day, it is."

Greg smiled (and uncrossed his fingers). "That explains all the people here on a Saturday. Will the records office be open?"

"To be sure! I'm going that way. I'll show you. Come along."

Robin was impressed with his easy friendliness and with the eager, helpfulness of those to whom he introduced them. They were left in the care of a student, one of many augmenting the staff during the festival, and, after showing identification, locating Sean Reilly's name turned out to be an easy task.

He had entered the university in 1962 and graduated in 1966. "With honors," Robin noted. She felt a little shaky. Just hearing his name read from an official document gave her chills. This was her *father*.

"But there's no mention of a wife," the student worker said. There was, in fact, nothing beyond his college record. Sean's address on entry was Reilly Castle, Ballylith. He stayed in a dormitory for two years, then moved off campus to an address in Belfast for the remaining time.

"At least there's an address," Greg said. "We'll go there."

"Before we do, let's see if there's anyone here who might remember him."

"That's more than thirty years ago, Robin. A long time."

"Maybe not."

The student ran a print-out of Sean's record, then delivered it into the hands of an older staff member, who scrutinized it carefully while protecting it from their inquisitive eyes.

"I've been here thirty-nine years," she said, shaking her head, "but with eight thousand students here now, and my advancing age," she added with a .smile, "I have a hard time remembering individuals. There's one instructor here, though, who may have taught that history class." She tapped the paper with her chubby finger, saying, "Mr. Stewart was new then." She looked up. "Now he's an institution."

~~~

The luck o' the Irish, Robin thought, as she and Greg took seats in Mr. Nigel Stewart's office. Mr. Stewart was in because of the festival; he was not conducting classes because of the festival, and he was glad that he had some time to spare for American visitors. They sat comfortably in armchairs facing his desk.

"So you're Sean Reilly's daughter," he said. He was an Englishman, the kind that Americans might call "stuffy" at first glance. His nose was long and straight, like his body and demeanor. Even after three decades of living and teaching in Ireland, he still spoke with the very distinctive, clipped English accent. "I came here to Queen's as Sean was entering his final year, so I didn't know him for a great length of time. However, I *do* remember him. Sean Reilly was a memorable young man."

"Mr. Stewart," Robin said, "I've only known for a short time that he was my father. Friends of the family believe that he is no longer living, but no one really knows what happened to him."

"In that respect, I'm afraid I'm not going to be much help either. After Sean left the university, I never heard from him again."

"I would appreciate very much anything you can tell me. Anything at all. You said he was memorable. In what way?"

Nigel Stewart smiled a tiny bit, as if more might crack his face. "You may not care to hear this, but Sean was what I believe you Americans call a...a 'hot-head.'" He cleared his throat.

"Relax, Mr. Stewart," said Greg with a grin. "Robin's a hot-head, too. It seems she inherited the trait."

Robin gave him a friendly poke. "I want to hear everything," she said.

"In that case, I'll continue. Would you care for a sweet?" he asked, pausing to offer a tin of Thornton's Fruit Sweets. They each accepted one of the lightly sugared, hard candies. Mr. Stewart put one in his mouth and rolled it with his tongue as he spoke. "Sean was a political activist. Absolutely thrived on dissention. If students were marching, Sean Reilly was in the front line; if there were a rally, he was a prominent speaker; if there were an argument in the classroom, his voice would be heard above the others. And, believe me, in our class on Irish history, there was plenty of argument."

"I know this must sound terribly naïve, even calloused and uncaring," Robin said, "but I don't understand what it is the Irish argue and fight about. The only thing I've heard is that Protestants and Catholics can't get along, and they fight in the name of religion. To me, that seems so unreasonable, so terrible, that maybe that's why I've kind of shut my ears to it all. It's too incredible. And I haven't really *wanted* to know...until now. Why did my father care so much?"

Mr. Stewart sat up a little straighter. "Oh, my dear child," he said, "there's much more to it than that. It's not simply Protestants against Catholics. It's a very complex situation and not one I can put in a...a nutshell, so to speak."

"Please try," Robin pleaded. "It means a lot to me."

He looked at her from beneath raised eyebrows. "In a nutshell, hmmm?"

She nodded, and he settled back in his chair.

"Well, then, let's begin with the fact that the great majority of Irish are Catholic. We're talking about *all* of Ireland now, the entire island. In Northern Ireland today, of course, the Protestants outnumber the Catholics two to one. But hundreds of years ago Catholic missionaries came to Ireland, offering religion where there was none at all. The people were hungry for it. Add to that, the fact that Ireland, in those early times, had no political unity, rather a host of tiny kingdoms in a time when social standing depended on property and possessions. Kings rose and fell in battles that were often little more than sport.

"Then, in the year 1169, a fallen Irish king enlisted the help of Henry II of England, a Protestant. Henry not only helped, he moved in and claimed lordship. The Irish resisted, and for the next several hundred years, what with intermarriage and mixed loyalties, the fighting over possession of land continued, this time involving the English and those loyal to the English." He paused. "Are you still with me?"

Robin nodded.

"It was Henry VIII who finally took enough notice of the situation to proclaim himself King of Ireland, 'by right of conquest,' he said. Then the English, asserting their authority, seized huge tracts of land in Ulster, that's Northern Ireland, and replaced the landowners with Protestants who were loyal to the crown. After twelve more years of war, they imposed Penal Law, denying Catholics property rights, the right to hold office, even the right to an education. Protestants who did not agree with this were likewise penalized. Now, remember what I said in the beginning, that the majority of Irish are Catholic. When this huge force finally rose, demanding independence, Britain yielded, but with a catch—though they would rule themselves, the Irish still would be under the British crown. This, of course, was unacceptable, but they managed a tenuous peace.

"Finally, in the early twentieth-century, those desiring an independent Republic of Ireland—the republicans—tried another ploy, a political one. They gained a majority of seats in government and declared Ireland a republic. British authorities, still the official government, proclaimed this illegal and drove the movement underground, where it continued to fester in secret.

"Inevitably, bitter fighting broke out. To settle it, a treaty was drawn, naming six counties of Ulster—the other two were not included—in union with Britain. The rest of Ireland became the Irish Free State with dominion status, which still was not acceptable. A civil war then erupted, separating the two parts of Ireland completely." Mr. Stewart paused again, helping himself to another candy and offering them to Robin and Greg.

"Today we have Northern Ireland, which is part of Great Britain, and the Republic of Ireland, which is completely independent. The problem is that Irish nationalists—and there are many on both sides—still want a united Ireland. They want to drive the British out and unite their country. Unfortunately, it appears to be a religious war because of the way the country is divided. Actually, it's a *political* war, doubly sad because it pits Catholic against Protestant, brother against brother. Believe it or not, there are Catholics and Protestants in Northern Ireland, and elsewhere on the isle, who live together peaceably."

"Forgive me, Mr. Stewart," Robin said. "I know you are English...but why don't the English just pull out and leave Ireland to the Irish?"

He smiled indulgently. "Remember the hundreds of years of intermarriage and mixed loyalties. There are good Irish Protestants who are proud to be part of Great Britain."

Robin sighed and leaned back in her chair. "That helps me picture my father more clearly. I can see him, just as you said—Sean Reilly at the head of a march, waving a flag of the Republic, screaming and shouting for Catholicism and a United Ireland. That's a Reilly all right!" She nodded to herself, smiling.

Mr. Stewart again cleared his throat. "Miss Reilly," he began, "I seem to have given you the wrong impression." He paused; clearly weighing his next words. "Sean Reilly was an activist for *Northern Ireland*. He converted to Protestantism."

CHAPTER 18

They held hands in the backseat of a taxi, heading for the house on Falls Road, Sean Reilly's last known address "I feel like a child, Greg," Robin said. "Every time I get up and try to walk, something knocks me down."

He lifted her hand and kissed it. "And I will always be there to help you up again."

Her face softened. "I love you," she whispered. "Oh, I *do* love you, so very much." She lay her head against his shoulder. "At least we've a good idea now why Sean was disowned. Can you imagine a Reilly from Ballylith becoming a *Protestant*? Even Patrick, who came from Belfast, was a firm Catholic. The words *Reilly* and *Catholic* are almost synonymous. I wonder if any of Sean's friends are still around."

"Don't pin your hopes on this address, Robin. More than thirty years ago? It's a long shot." His eyes were scanning the streets. He was concerned about the taxi driver's wary response to the destination: "You sure, mister?"

"Mr. Stewart didn't want us to follow up on it. What did he say—that we'd be 'uncomfortable' in the area. As if I cared about comfort!"

She would soon reconsider her words. At the entrance to Falls Road, their taxi abruptly pulled over and stopped at a parking lot filled with old black London taxicabs.

"Where are we?" she asked, sitting up straight.

"Falls Road. This is as far as I go, miss," the driver said. "One of the Black Cabs will take you the rest of the way."

"Why?"

"Because the Black Cabs can go up the Falls Road without being attacked." He got out and opened the back door. "Enjoy your trip, folks."

Robin swallowed hard, clutched Greg's hand, then said very quickly, "Don't even suggest turning back, Greg. I'm going on, with or without you."

"*With* me!"

~~~

Their Black Cab moved slowly up the road, giving them plenty of time to take in the old bombed-out flats, the graffiti-covered walls, teenagers with vacant eyes...and the children. Children "playing" with a car—kicking in the sides, smashing windows. Children no more than eight to ten years old. Robin gasped involuntarily.

"They'll torch it when they're done, they will," said the driver. "It's all part of the game, copying the big boys." He turned into a housing project and up to a string of row houses. "Here we are," he said, stopping in front of the number Greg had provided.

Robin sat, dumbfounded. The scene was, to say the least, bleak. And in total contrast to downtown Belfast. It was like another world, lonely and poor. Adding to the sense of desolation, clouds had covered the sun, releasing the heavy, perpetual mist. She hugged her windbreaker closer to her body.

A little boy, no more than seven or eight years old, red-haired and freckled, sat on the front stoop next door. He was smoking a cigarette, watching covertly through the curls of smoke. In the house they sought, a curtain stirred, revealing an old woman. Someone was home.

Greg was the first to move. He helped Robin out then paid the cab driver. With a generous tip he extracted a promise that the driver would wait. As he and Robin navigated the broken walk to the stoop, the front door opened.

The old woman was wary but curious. "Nobody's home," she said.

Greg smiled. "You're home. Would you talk with us?"

"What about?"

"About someone who used to live here, about thirty-five or -six years ago."

"I moved here twelve years ago."

Robin couldn't conceal her disappointment. Her shoulders sagged.

"Before that," the woman said, "I lived next door."

Robin's eyes brightened.

"Lived there twelve years, too."

"Maybe you know someone who can help us," Greg suggested.

"Before I lived next door, I lived across the street. Lived there a little more'n twelve years."

If there were such a thing as "patient exasperation," it would describe Robin perfectly. She wanted to throw something. Anything! Instead, she said, gently, "May we come inside and talk with you? We need to locate someone who used to live in this house."

The woman looked both of them up and down, then peered left and right to see who might be watching. Then she did an odd thing. She hissed at the child next door. He rose, tossed his cigarette into the street, yelled, in his very young voice, "Ah, fug off!" and went inside his own building.

"There'll be no trouble from that one," she said. "He's bone-lazy anyway." She stood aside, holding the door open.

Robin shook her head in dismay. *He's just a child,* she thought, stepping across the threshhold. The room was cold and sparsely furnished but clean. The air smelled of stale cabbage. She offered them chairs around a center table and took one for herself. "Who y' after knowing about?" she asked.

Robin was still speechless, so Greg answered for her. "Sean Reilly," he said. "He was a student at the university. The officer there told us that he lived in this house sometime during the middle nineteen-sixties. You would have been across the street then. Do you remember him?"

The old woman answered slowly. "I'd have to be a dimwit not to. A real rabble-rouser he was there at the end; well, actually *she* was. And we were nice to them, too. Him and that Fiona Morrison. Not even married, they weren't. But livin' together."

Robin felt her heart skip a beat.

"Him Catholic and her Protestant," the woman continued, "at least that's the way it was for a while. We lived peaceable down here, Catholics and Protestants mixed up some, but then Sean crossed over, and *she* wasn't satisfied with livin' peaceable. Had to parade their politics, they did. Caused some big trouble, and the smoke of battle still stings me eyes. What else you want to know about him?"

With effort, Robin found her voice. "Uh, ma'am," she started.

"Mrs. Corcoran."

"Mrs. Corcoran, Sean Reilly was my father, but I never knew him. I'm trying to find out what became of him. Where did he go from here? Do you know?"

"Ah, now, come to think of it, you do look a little like him." She squinted at Robin. "His hair was a wee bit darker."

"Do you know where he went? Did he leave a forwarding address?"

Mrs. Corcoran laughed aloud, revealing a broken front tooth. "Forwarding address, is it? Not that one. He snuck off in the night, he did, him and that Fiona Morrison. Too many enemies." She laughed again. "Forwarding address!"

Robin tried again. "Would he have gone back into the city? Into Belfast?"

But Mrs. Corcoran seemed not to have heard. She was staring at a crack in the wall. Then she said, "I stayed 'cause I thought things would get better. But they only got worse."

It was Greg's turn. "Did Sean Reilly have friends that you remember?"

Mrs. Corcoran scratched her head then reached down to scratch her leg. Her ankles looked as if they were covered in chigger bites, but Robin didn't know if Ireland had chiggers.

"Seems to me Sean mentioned they'd be livin' in Derry," Mrs. Corcoran said. "That's where that Fiona Morrison came from." Suddenly the old woman's voice rose to a screech, startling Robin nearly out of her chair. "Derry! Protestant Ulster's Holy City!" She spat out the phrase with disdain. Even her capital letters were audible. Then she added, quietly, "That's all I know."

"You've been very helpful, Mrs. Corcoran," Robin said. "We'll look for them in Londonderry."

"Derry! 'Tis *Derry!* Only bloody English sympathizers call ancient Derry by that hateful London name!"

Robin swallowed. "Sorry."

"That's all right, dear. You didn't know any better." She gestured toward the open kitchen. "Sorry I can't offer you a proper tea. Don't have any."

Robin and Greg both stood and thanked her. "We appreciate your talking with us," Robin said. At least now she had a name and a city—Fiona Morrison and... yes, *Derry*. Two more things to check on.

Outside on the front stoop, Greg pressed money into Mrs. Corcoran's palm. "This is for tea," he said with a wink. "Buy some for your next guests."

"Me next guests, is it?" Mrs. Corcoran's hearty laugh could surely be heard throughout the project. It drew the boy next door back outside to scrutinize Robin and Greg as they walked toward the street. "Well, I'll not be turning it down!" the woman called into the thickening mist.

At the edge of the broken sidewalk, the Black Cab waited silently, motor turned off. Like a cat without a purr.

CHAPTER 19

Robin sat in their hotel room, hugging Wrenny's rag doll. The experience in "the flats" had left her shaken.

"Why the children, Greg? Why are the children not children at all? This isn't their war. It wasn't Wrenny's war. Nor mine." A tear rolled down her cheek.

Greg stood by the window, looking out. "The soldiers were there, Robin. We didn't see them, but they were there. The children have grown up with them. In that area it's all they know. I remember reading that in 1989, on the twentieth anniversary of the uprising, a group of children hijacked two buses and a truck and set fire to them. A fifteen-year-old boy was killed. It goes on, Robin. On and on."

He turned to face her, leaning on the windowsill. "Something else you must realize," he said, kindly, "is that the area we went into is not one of a kind. We'll be leaving for Londonderry soon. That's where Northern Ireland's recent history of war began. And given Sean Reilly's involvement in Irish politics, what we find there may be even more unsettling."

"What did Mrs. Corcoran mean when she called Derry a Holy Protestant City, or something to that effect? She sounded like she was swearing."

"I've never been to Derry, but I understand that it's partly a walled city. Has been since the seventeenth-century when the Protestants built a huge, stone wall to shut out the Catholic peasants. Even though people travel in and out today, the wall is a bitter reminder. And for the most part, the Catholics still live outside the wall in the boglands. They call that area Bogside. And Robin...it's another ghetto."

~~~

Robin was sure she couldn't eat a bite of "afternoon tea," but Greg insisted she try. It had been a long time since breakfast. It was a lavish spread: wheaten bread, sweet bannocks, crusty baps (buns), treacle farls, and potato farls—

triangular goodies baked on a griddle. There was also a plate of scones with cream and Mourne honey. Greg ate ravenously, and soon Robin found herself doing the same, surprised that she was suddenly so hungry.

After tea they shopped for souvenirs. Robin found a beautiful length of double damask linen for Cassie and a pretty belt for Wrenny. Greg bought some light-weight tweed for his grandmother and a blackthorn walking stick for himself. "I'll look at it until I'm old," he said, "then I'll put it to good use!"

Outside on the street, they enjoyed a band of street musicians playing fiddles and a bodhrán, the traditional Irish goatskin drum.

By this time, Robin's spirits had lifted considerably, and Greg felt it prudent to leave Belfast immediately. His excuse to Robin was to use the remaining daylight for a head start to Londonderry, or "Derry." While he was checking out of their hotel and arranging for their car to be brought around, Robin called ahead for reservations at a small bed-and-breakfast inn just off the main route on the edge of the Sperrin Mountains. In a very short time they were on their way out the M2, toward Derry.

The volume of traffic was low; though the speed limit was 70 mph, they still had to drive on the left-hand side of the motorway. This alone encouraged them to keep their speed in the fifties. It was fortunate that the road was well-surfaced and well-posted.

Then came a change in the weather. For the worse. The day that had begun sunny and clear had clouded into a drizzly rain. As darkness approached, they were barely able to see the gentle contours of the Sperrins, the vast moorland, and the whitewashed cottages snuggled up to sycamore trees. Through the gloom, lamplit windows twinkled.

Mrs. Doherty's Bed and Breakfast Inn

~~~

It wasn't until morning that Robin and Greg were able to appreciate the charm of their inn. They woke up in a high, four-poster in a spotlessly clean room, made homey with hand-sewn bedding and rugs. There were fresh flowers on a corner table, and the window was open just a tiny bit, enough to let in the clean, country air.

Robin climbed out of bed and pushed the window all the way up. "Oh, look, Greg. Come, look!" she cried. "Peacocks!"

There were three, strutting and posing on the green lawn beyond the window. The sun was just peeking over the horizon, coaxing the wet grass to sparkle. And Greg, looking at Robin's bright face, was glad that the experience in Belfast was behind them.

Breakfast was served by their friendly hostess in a modest dining room near the kitchen. Mrs. Doherty, aptly named, was shaped like a pudgy ball of dough. Her thighs rubbed together as she walked, her thick stockings going "swish-swish, swish-swish." Kevin, her seven-year-old grandson, "helped" cook and serve the meal.

"Your home is lovely," Robin commented as she tasted the rainbow trout. She'd never eaten trout for breakfast.

"'Twas a rectory in its day, dear. Been standin' for exactly two hundred years, and the peat fire's never gone out in all that time," she said proudly.

"It hasn't?"

"Oh, no. If the peat fire goes out, life itself may go out o' those who live in the house. 'Tis an old superstition, but I'm worried enough to keep the fire burning."

"That's amazing! Two hundred years?"

Mrs. Doherty nodded. "'Course regular heating and plumbing were added in our time, and me husband Ian and me, we've done a grayut amount o' work on the inside to make it comfy."

Robin couldn't help but notice her accent, much different from the folks of Ballylith. There was still a lilt, but the pronunciation was broader, and the sentences ended in an upward inflection, much as in the southern United States.

"You've done a wonderful job," Robin said. "By the way, we appreciated the fresh flowers."

Mrs. Doherty smiled. "Kevin here cut them from what used to be the churchyard. Church was down the road, but it didn't last like the house. 'Tis gone now, all but the graves."

Kevin piped up. "Would ye like to see them? The graves? I cud take ye there?"

"Thank you, no," Greg answered, noting the disappointment on Kevin's face. The boy had no doubt anticipated a few pence in his pocket. "We have to leave right after breakfast. Maybe you could help me load the car in a little while."

The child's eyes brightened. "Sure, mister!"

"Ah, now, won't ye stay the day?" Mrs. Doherty asked. "We've beautiful country here in the Sperrins, and I've two good bicycles in the shed to loan ye."

Robin smiled. "Thank you, but we have business to take care of in Lon— uh, Derry. It can't wait."

"Derry, eh? Ye're not far from there now, ye know, just a short drive. Ye'll like Derry. 'Tis a nice city. Good shopping, though Sunday is hardly the day to be going. Business is it?"

"We're, uh, going to see someone. Ac-actually, some relatives," Robin explained, not too satisfactorily.

"Folks, now? Mebbe I know them. Me husband Ian and me, we're farmers, that's why he had breakfast much earlier than you, y' see—I'm real sorry you won't be meetin' him; he's a real looker, he is—and we go to Derry often for supplies. Go to church there, too. Presbyterian. We know lots o' folks."

"Well, uh...." Robin cleared her throat, thinking quickly. "They're Morrisons. Probably lots of Morrisons in Derry," she added with a self-conscious shrug.

"Sure 'n that's a fact. Presbyterians, too. Now what Morrisons would ye be looking for?"

Robin felt a little foolish. How could she answer?

Greg saved her the trouble. "The family's been around for a lot of years," he explained. "There was a young woman named Fiona Morrison, who, I understand, was active in politics about thirty years ago. I'm not sure we'll be able to locate them, but—" He stopped. Mrs. Doherty's mouth had popped open.

"Mrs. Doherty?"

"Oh, now," Mrs. Doherty said on an exhalation of breath. "It's Fiona Morrison's folks ye're wantin', is it?" She rose abruptly and lifted the coffee pot off the flame on the sideboard. "Would ye like a warm-up, dear? Coffee's always on the perkie in this house."

"Please," Robin replied.

The lady refilled all three cups and replaced the pot. "Y' say ye are… *relatives?*" She twisted her apron in her fingers.

"Very distantly," Greg quickly injected, picking up on her sudden nervousness. "We're just curious about the family, what became of everyone, you know the kind of thing." He gave the "grand shrug" he had learned in Ireland, making his words sound unimportant.

Mrs. Doherty exhaled another "Oh, now," and leaned against the sideboard. "Ye must be tracin' yer roots. Sure 'n ye Americans like to trace yer roots!" She seemed instantly more relaxed. "For a minute there I thought I was entertainin' one of *the* Morrisons. Lord in heaven above knows my wee place isn't fine enough for that!"

"Is, uh, is Fiona Morrison still alive, Mrs. Doherty?" Robin asked.

"Fiona? Mercy, no! And probably a good thing it is, too, for all she was so radical there at the end. Fact is, a sniper's bullet got her during one o' her wild speeches. That was, let's see, 'round early nineteen-seventies it was. Yer not read in Irish history, are ye?"

"Well, no," Robin answered apologetically. "We just decided to do this on the spur of the moment. The reason we want to go to Derry today," she added, including young Kevin in her explanation, "is that our vacations will be ending soon. We'd like to learn as much as possible before it's time to leave for America."

Greg was amazed at Robin's calm façade. She had just learned that her own mother was killed by a sniper, yet she showed no emotion. Had she shed all of her tears for Wrenny and the children of Belfast? Were there none left?

"I guess what you find out," Mrs. Doherty offered, "depends on how far back you want to go. Probably the Presbyterian registry would have the information—not the wee church *my* family attends, understand, but the *big* one." She nodded knowingly.

"Would you happen to know the names of Fiona's parents, Mrs. Doherty?" Greg asked. Robin thanked him silently. Beneath her calm exterior, every bone in her body was shaking.

"Everyone knows that. *The* Morrisons, Daniel and Delia, may they rest in peace."

"They're…not living?"

She shook her head. "No. They died before Fiona got carried away with herself, and that's mebbe a blessing, too. I'm not sure they would have liked the way things were turning." She turned and poured a cup of coffee for herself. "Now they were good Protestants and supported London 'n all, like Fiona, don't get me wrong, but they were not violent people. It was said that Mrs. Morrison, Delia, was a quiet little thing, sickly. Not what you'd expect from people with all that money."

"What did their money come from?" Greg asked.

"The Shop, of course. *Morrison's.* I believe you call them department stores in America." Then she added in tones of hushed awe, "Think of them as the Department Store Morrisons. *Fine* folks."

Daniel and Delia Morrison, according to Mrs. Doherty, had inherited a tiny clothing store from Daniel's father and built it into an empire—the largest "shop" in Londonderry, with catalog sales all over Europe. It was called, simply, *Morrison's.* Fiona, however, their only child, was not interested in the business, except as it financed her political activities.

"She was a good lass, Fiona was," said Mrs. Doherty. "Well-intentioned, but a wee bit wild with her political ways, if y' know what I mean. A real speechmaker, she was. Could stir the people into a mighty frenzy, which more than once came to no good. I, for one, believe in our government, too, with me whole heart; but I'm not comfortable with making all of Ireland see it our way." She shifted her body and sighed. "I'm weary of war 'n all."

"Mrs. Doherty, do you know anything about Fiona's husband?"

"Husband?" She thought a moment. "Seems to me she did marry, but I don't know...say, now! She married a Reilly! Isn't that your name, lass— Reilly?" Robin nodded mutely. "Can't say as I heard what happened to him. Things were so bad in those days. People out o' work. Skirmishes. Throwing things—nails, stones, then petrol bombs. Gunfire right in the streets of Derry, there was." Her words got slower and softer, almost hushed. "Tanks, armored cars. The British troops, they tried to quash it, but.... " She lifted her apron to the corner of one eye, then said quickly, "Me husband Ian and me, we mostly stayed home back then."

Greg rose. "You've been very helpful, Mrs. Doherty," he said. "Kevin, how about helping me load the car? Meet me outside in ten minutes."

"Sure, mister!" The boy bounded out of the room.

"Are you all right?" Greg asked Robin once they were back in their room.

"Fine," she replied, twisting away from him, her chin jutting into the air. "There isn't another thing I could possibly learn that would surprise me." Her eyes flashed. "My system is numb from shock, Greg! First, I don't have parents; then, I have parents; then, they're Protestants, not Catholics; then, they're radical activists." She started slamming things into her suitcase.

"Now I find that my mother was gunned down by a sniper because she was some kind of violent nut case! What does that make me? *What*, Greg?"

"Robin, stop it."

"No, I won't stop it! I'm sick of 'stopping it.' It's been one thing after another, after another, and I'm supposed to sit quietly and smile sweetly and say, 'Oh, gee whiz, so that's the way it was.' Well, I'm not a 'gee whiz' person, Greg. I'm *me*! And I'm mad as hell! I feel like I'm on both ends of a tug of war. Sean and Fiona were very different from each other, and together they were *extremely* different from Ronan and Maeve. Patrick wasn't like any of them, but he didn't want me to find out any of this, God only knows why. Wrenny is different, and it's not her fault. And you're different from me, too, Greg. It's like we're walking down the same track but out of step. You're Protestant, I'm Catholic; you're a preservationist, I'm a killer; you're kind and gentle, I'm quick-tempered and probably not fit to have children. Just look what Fiona, my *mother*, did with hers!"

"Robin, stop. Look at me!" Greg caught hold of her shoulders and squeezed them until he got her attention. "Anyone on this earth has the potential for violence. I do. Or Cassie or Jerome. Or my grandmother…given a motive or provocation. Do you understand me, Robin? There's nothing wrong with temper, as long as you don't let it control you. *You* be the controller. A burst of temper doesn't *reason*, and most of all, it has no patience. Solutions to problems usually come to us, Robin, when we've exercised a little patience."

"Are you being *patient* with me now?" she snapped.

"Yes. Because I love you. And don't think you're the only one who notices *our* differences. I notice them, too, and sometimes, like now, it scares me. But it also excites me because accepting these differences and giving each other 'breathing room' is a challenge." He relaxed his hold and gently stroked her shoulders. "Our love is special, Robin. It's a *precious gem*. Not a rough one, but one of many beautifully cut facets."

Robin quickly shut her eyes against stinging tears as Greg enfolded her in his arms. While he held her, her anger slowly diffused, and she began to realize just how much of her strength and her courage now came from him.

~~~

A short time later they stood near their car with Mrs. Doherty and Kevin. The child had several new pence in his pocket and a broad grin on his chubby-cheeked face. A neighbor, Tupper O'Toole, had stopped to pass the time of day and was now bicycling on down the road.

"He seems like a nice fellow," Robin said, watching him go.

"Oh, Tupper's fine, 'cept he digs with the other foot," Mrs. Doherty replied. "Now there's me phone ringing. 'Bye to y' both and drop in again one day," she said, swish-swishing very quickly toward the bright blue door of her house.

"What did she mean by that?" Greg asked Kevin. "'He digs with the other foot.'"

"Oh, he's Catholic."

~~~

As they left the peace and tranquility of the country inn, Robin said, "I never told her I was Catholic."

"It wouldn't have mattered. She's a good woman."

CHAPTER 20

As Robin and Greg drove across the River Foyle via the Craigavon Bridge, the ancient walls of Londonderry were an imposing sight though the walls by no means encompassed the modern city of Derry. Many shops and businesses prospered outside the walls, and gracious country homes of wealthy citizens overlooked the river. Like all of Ireland's communities, Derry was religious, whatever the persuasion, and this aspect of Irish life certainly made itself known on this bright, sunshiny Sunday morning. The streets were quiet.

Robin hoped that at some point, possibly by evening, she could find a place to slip unobtrusively into Mass; if not that, then perhaps a parish priest would hear her confession. She needed to be absolved of the bad feelings she'd had about Patrick and Anna, particularly Patrick, and of those she continued to have about Sean and Fiona. And Ronan. She did not understand Ronan. If she could just see the whole picture, perhaps she could forgive the Reillys and *the* Morrisons for what had happened to her and Wrenny, especially to Wrenny. She needed the means to forgive them before she could expect forgiveness for herself.

"What is it?" Greg asked.

Robin shook her head to clear the confusion. "Still the same thing. I've got to get it straightened out or I'll be an emotional wreck the rest of my life."

"Isn't that what we're doing? Straightening it out?"

Robin said kindly, "I'm sorry, Greg. I could never have handled this on my own. I had no idea our trip to Ireland would lead to this…this emotional upheaval! I thought I'd have a few sharp words with Mr. O'Sullivan, find my birthplace, do a little sightseeing and go home. But a *search*, for heaven's sake!" She signed heavily. "Greg, thank you, thank you for being with me. I appreciate it more than you can possibly know. But I am *truly* sorry that you're losing so much time away from your work, your coffee-table book."

"Quit being sorry. I'm enjoying the role of Sherlock Holmes. Besides, you'll notice the camera is never far from my side." That was true. As they'd driven through Ireland, he'd stopped the car from time to time to take "shots," and he'd also enjoyed shooting Mrs. Doherty's peacocks.

She moved closer to him. "Just so you don't put that camera between us."

"Don't get too close," he warned. "I'm still not used to the steering wheel on the right side, and you're a distraction." He managed a wink with his left eye.

"My father—Patrick, that is—taught me an old Irish blessing. It goes like this: 'May the road rise to meet you. May the wind be always at your back. May the sun shine warm upon your face, and the rains fall soft upon your fields. And may I always distract you, that we'll never part again.'"

"You changed the ending."

"I did?"

"Even I know that one."

"Well, now, an' maybe ye don't know this one, Mister Smarty. 'Wishing you always—walls for the wind and a roof for the rain, and tea beside the fire. Laughter to cheer you, and those you love near you, and all that your heart might desire.'"

"All?"

"All."

"You're distracting me again. Look, there's a man on that next corner. I'll pull up and ask directions."

"Directions to what?"

"The Presbyterian Church, of course. The *big* one."

"I hope he's not selling sweetbreads and cruibins."

~~~

It was twelve o'clock noon when they parked across the street from the church. Bells chimed as the Presbyterians descended the steps, hurrying to their cars in the parking lot. Robin wondered if they were trying to beat the Catholics to the restaurants for Sunday dinner as the Methodists always raced the Baptists in Florida.

"What do we do now?" she asked.

"We wait until the pastor is the only one left; then, we ask him about *the* Morrisons."

"Right, Sherlock."

His name was Christopher Grogan. He was tall and thin with a head full of white hair and a face full of smile. At first glance his teeth seemed longer than his nose. Only a slight hesitancy in his walk indicated that he might be older than he looked.

"Thirty years isn't such a long time when ye'r my age," he said. "Problem is, I wasn't in Derry then. Called, I was, from Country Antrim."

"But you've heard of the Morrisons?"

"Of course. I shop at their store. And anyone read in Irish history knows of Fiona." He sat in a big, comfortable chair behind his office desk. Robin and Greg sat in straight-backed, uncomfortable chairs in front of the desk. Not conducive to long visits. "No Morrisons here now, not that family, I mean."

"Is there anyone who might help us? We're interested in learning anything we can about Fiona and her husband, Sean Reilly." Robin felt as if she were pleading, but if that's what it took, that's what she'd do. A bit nervous, she pushed her hair behind her ears, unaware of the gesture.

Christopher Grogan scratched his head. "Well, now, there's a woman in this congregation who claims to have been Fiona's best friend. Doesn't come to church much."

"How can we find her?"

He reached to the corner of his desk and flipped through a rolling index of his membership. "Here she is," he said, isolating a card. "Anngret Fahey. Don't expect much, though. She keeps to herself. Eccentric. Has a slight turn in the eye."

Robin's nervousness once again turned to excitement—*so many ups and downs!* Greg copied the address and phone number, and they both thanked the Reverend Grogan and quickly stood. Robin's body ached from just five minutes on that hard chair.

~~~

Unable to reach Anngret Fahey by phone, Robin and Greg drove to the address Grogan had given them, an expensive Georgian townhouse within the walls of Old Derry. Since it was mealtime, they didn't try the door, just scouted the area for a later return.

"Let's take a walk around the walls," Greg suggested. "Maybe she'll be home by the time we finish."

Robin hadn't realized that they could actually walk on top of the ancient walls, but it was so. The walls had been standing since their completion in 1618, still unbroken. From such a commanding height, they could see the inner city's medieval plan, still intact—four principal streets radiating from a central square called "The Diamond," and several smaller streets twisting beneath the shadow of the walls. Originally, the walls were entered through four arch-gates, one for each of the four main streets, but now there were seven gates to accommodate more traffic. Robin located the area where Anngret Fahey lived, but she could not pinpoint the townhouse from such a distance.

It took them an hour to walk the walls, stopping now and then to look at the cannons and bastions. They also looked beyond the walls, to the Foyle estuary, the famous Guildhall, the green hillside, and Bogside, the Catholic ghetto. It was all very quaint; it was authentic; it was sad; it was frightening.

"Let's find that cathedral," Robin said as they drove their rented car once again inside the walls. "It was so beautiful from up there. Maybe they'll have posted a schedule of services."

"I don't think it's what you're looking for," Greg replied.

"Why not?"

"That was St. Columb's. It's Anglican."

"Oh. Well, let's find it anyway. It was pretty."

When they found the lovely building, they also found a stone inscription in its porch. Robin read aloud:

If stones could speake
Then London's prayse
Should sounde who
Built this church and
Cittie from the grounde.

A definite reminder that they stood on British soil.

~~~

Robin finally reached Anngret Fahey by phone at 5:00 p.m. and was delighted to hear a warm, friendly, musical voice on the other end of the line. Mrs. Fahey was pleased, even eager, to meet Robin Reilly.

"May we take you out for Sunday supper?" Robin offered. "We could talk over a good meal."

"Oh, no, dear. I have an excellent cook, and we'll be much more comfortable here in my own home. Could you come around, say, seven o'clock? Then we'll have plenty of time to chat."

"Yes, of course," Robin answered, thinking that they could easily be there in ten minutes. Delay was agony, but after all, she and Greg were the intruders. "We'll be there at seven."

They used the extra time to register at a hotel, clean up a bit and change clothes.

"I don't know what to wear!" Robin cried as she unpacked her suitcase.

"Anything you want to. We're tourists. She'll make allowances for us."

Robin rolled her eyes. "Men!" She agonized over choices for nearly twenty minutes before deciding. By that time Greg was ready and had picked up the TV remote.

Robin looked at the remote and, once again, said, "Men!"

~~~

At precisely seven o'clock, they tapped the brass doorknocker. "Greg, I'm starving!" Robin whispered as they waited. "That 'ploughman's lunch' didn't hold me very well. It was *good* bread and *good* cheese, but still just bread and cheese."

"I thought you liked traditional food."

"I'm getting weary of it. What I wouldn't give for a hamburger and fries!"

The door opened then, and Anngret Fahey greeted her guests with open arms. "Oh, my goodness!" she cried, hugging Robin. "You have your father's nose and your mother's hair, and let's see, yes, her chin! Oh, I can't tell you how glad I am to see you!"

The woman was petite with dark, walnut-colored hair cut short and lifted to frame her face with soft curls. The "slight turn in her eye," that Christopher Grogan had spoken of was slight indeed, just enough to make her extremely beautiful and unusual-looking, like one of Robin's favorite American film stars. She was richly dressed in a turquoise caftan, and Robin was glad she had worn her light wool dress with matching jacket. This was not a place for sweatsuits and Reebok shoes! Several strands of find gold chain hung from the lady's neck. Hardly what Robin had expected from the Reverend Grogan's description. *Eccentric? Keeps to herself?*

Mrs. Fahey guided her guests into a large sitting room with comfortable white furniture. The walls were white, the carpet was white, the draperies were made of white velvet, the huge grandfather clock now striking the hour was white. *Well, maybe just a touch eccentric.*

The room was chilly except for the area around the fireplace where they were invited to sit. The table in front of them held a carafe of hot punch, which Mrs. Fahey poured into tiny china cups. Robin was the first to taste it, and only good manners kept her from crying aloud. It was spiked, strongly enough to make up for the lack of heat in the room!

"What's in it?" she asked with a smile that found root in her toenails.

"Poteen, my dear." Mrs. Fahey leaned toward them with a secretive smile and whispered, "I make it myself!"

"M-Moonshine?"

"Is that what you call it in America? I mix it with lemonade, cloves and brown sugar. Do you like it?"

"Very much," Greg answered, grinning. He meant it.

Anngret Fahey was a widow. She had married late in life and had enjoyed the company of her husband for only three years before he died. Before and since her marriage, she had lived in this same townhouse with a cook-maid to care for her needs. She assured Robin and Greg that Lorna was even now cooking supper in the kitchen though Robin could smell nothing.

It took little encouragement for Mrs. Fahey to talk about Fiona Morrison. They had been best friends throughout their adolescent years, through the years at the Queen's University, and during the turbulent years leading to Fiona's death.

"Your mother was very attractive and extremely intelligent," she said. "No one could ask for a more loyal friend. When she was killed, I felt I had lost part of myself." She sighed. "But she was headstrong, and I think now, looking back on it all, a bit misguided. Her life was her politics. I'm sorry to be saying this, but politics came before everything—even before Sean and you and your sister. Oh, she loved Sean in her way. Fact is, he unknowingly provided petrol for her political fire. When he lost his arm during the march on Burntollet Bridge in January of sixty-nine, her passion for the cause became personal and much more violent. She couldn't see the folly of it. Then, when he was killed in August of that same year—the Battle of Bogside that's called now—she turned into a wild person, downright dangerous, particularly when she learned several weeks later that Wrenny's injury during that same battle would cause permanent disability. She had already sent you to Ronan, so, when Wrenny was out of hospital, she sent her, too. That left Fiona free to pursue her revenge. 'Twas no wonder she was shot down. She was stirring all of Northern Ireland into a fine frenzy."

Mrs. Fahey paused and looked directly, and kindly, at Robin. "Your mother did love you and Wrenny, you know. In her own strange way she loved you. My dear, are you sure you're wanting to hear this?"

Robin's eyes were damp. "I *need* to hear it, Mrs. Fahey. I need it *very much*. Did you know my father well?"

"Oh, yes!" She smiled, and her eyes took on new light. "He was handsome, intelligent, strong, gentle...everything one looks for in a man." She glanced at Greg. "His problem was, he was *too* much in love with your mother, if you can imagine such a thing. He hadn't her passion for politics, but he went along because he loved her. As I said, with Fiona, politics came first. With Sean, Fiona came first. If it hadn't been for her, he would most probably have gone back to the Republic and lived a very different life. As a Catholic." Mrs. Fahey blinked rapidly, fighting tears of her own. "He would have *lived*."

Greg reached for the poteen punch and refilled Mrs. Fahey's cup. Robin held hers toward him, and reluctantly, he refilled hers, too. He glanced at his watch. It was eight-thirty. Still no sign of supper.

"Mrs. Fahey," Robin began, "do you know why Sean left Reilly Castle and went to Belfast? Why did he choose Queen's rather than University College Dublin?"

Anngret Fahey smiled. "Because he wanted to see for himself what was happening to his country, to his Ireland. He was curious. His intention was to spend one year at Queen's then transfer back to the Republic, to Dublin. 'Twas a good plan." She drained her punch cup. "But he met Fiona. That was the beginning and end of it."

"Are any of Fiona's family members still living?"

"No. She was an only child. Inherited controlling stock in *Morrison's*, she did. That's the big shop on Shipquay Street. But she sold it all when she realized Wrenny wouldn't recover. That money—an enormous sum—was what she used to set up the trust funds."

"Funds?" Robin's face registered disbelief. "I knew about Wrenny's. There's another one?"

"Yes, of course, dear—yours. They're both administered by some solicitor down in Tralee. Haven't you been drawing on it?"

"It's possible," Robin answered, remembering the ease with which Patrick had paid for her education at Florida State University and for all the nice things she'd had growing up. She hadn't thought much about it at the time, but his salary was hardly enough to cover that kind of expense. One more thing to settle with young Mr. O'Sullivan.

Greg stood and moved to the fireplace, rubbing his hands, hoping a little motion would remind the lady that supper was overdue. He looked at Robin over his shoulder. She was pouring another cup of poteen punch and looking a tad giddy. *If she doesn't eat something soon*, he thought, *she'll have one hell of a hangover*!

But supper didn't come. Mrs. Fahey talked of Ireland, of Londonderry, of the "quiz evenings" at Dungloe Bar, of the shops on Shipquay Street, of Donegal tweeds and Carrickmacross lace.

At ten o'clock she rose and invited her guests to follow her to the dining room. Supper was ready. Greg helped Robin to her feet. And helped her walk to the dining room.

Lorna served, announcing, "Right on time," then left the room.

You mean just in time, Greg thought, seating Robin.

Each plate held little "balls of flour" potatoes, boiled onions and a meat that looked, well, interesting.

Greg tasted his meat. "That's good," he said. "Do you mind if I ask what it is?"

Mrs. Fahey beamed. "It's parma ham wrapped around loin of anglerfish."

Robin giggled.

~~~

"She was in love with Sean," Greg said as they lay in the darkness of their hotel bed.

"I know."

"It must have been difficult for her, being Fiona's best friend."

"I like her, Greg. She's a little strange, but I really like her."

"Anyone who's been through what she's been through has a right to be a little strange," he said. "Think of it—the fighting, the bombing, maiming, dying."

"And to be young and in love with a man who loves someone else, to watch him die for something he never should have been involved in. For nothing! I don't think I like Fiona very much," Robin said. "I'd have a hard time calling someone like that 'Mother.'" She stared into the darkness for a few moments. "No one ever called her Fiona Reilly, that's what Mrs. Fahey said. Always Fiona Morrison, even though they did marry after leaving Belfast."

"She was a woman ahead of her time. Maybe if she'd lived in our liberated days, she wouldn't have seemed so radical."

"I don't really care to know any more about her," Robin said, dismissing Fiona. "It's Sean that I wish I'd known."

"Did you like the anglerfish?"

"No. Greg, were you aware that suppertime up in these parts is ten o'clock at night? The truth, now. Did you let me starve on purpose?"

"I learned it the same way you did—hour by agonizing hour."

~~~

The phone rang at seven o'clock the next morning, and Robin responded with a groggy "Hello."

"Oh, dear, I've wakened you," said Anngret Fahey. "I apologize, but I was so afraid you'd get away and I wouldn't know where you'd gone."

Robin sat up in bed. "Is something wrong, Mrs. Fahey?"

"No, not wrong. It's…well, I've been awake most of the night thinking, trying to decide what to do. I want to show you something, Robin, and I…I want to give you something. When were you planning to leave Ulster?"

"There's no hurry. Would you like us to come to your house?"

"No, dear. I'll be at your hotel at nine o'clock. Is that too early? Do you mind going for a drive with me? Greg, too, of course."

"That will be fine. We'll be ready."

They dressed for a cold, foggy day.

~~~

Anngret Fahey was a competent driver, at ease on the twisting roads outside of Derry. They had crossed the River Foyle and turned off the main motorway, following a narrow country road. In a few moments she turned again, this time into a small cemetery, heavy with mist. They got out of the car and walked down a pathway between graves, coming at last to two small headstones, side by side, on the edge of a grassy knoll. The first read, "Sean, 1944-1969," and the second, "Fiona, 1944-1972." No surnames.

Tears stung Robin's eyes, then trickled through her lashes as she clutched Greg's arm.

"Since Sean had no family," Mrs. Fahey said, "other than his uncle and aunt—the Ronan Reillys, who weren't wanting him—I suggested to Fiona that he be buried here. Quietly and without fuss. Then when Fiona died, it seemed logical to bring her here, too. I thought you should know."

"Thank you," Robin whispered. She was overcome, not only by the reality and finality of her parents' graves, but by the kind and generous gesture of Anngret Fahey in sharing something that had been hers, privately, for more than thirty years. She alone had known where the graves were located. She alone had known the surnames missing from the headstones.

After a few moments Mrs. Fahey pulled a small package from the pocket of her coat. "I want you to have this," she said, handing it to Robin. "It belonged to your father."

Robin carefully unfolded the tissue. Inside was a most unusual rosary.

"Sean bought it when he first arrived at Queen's before he met Fiona. It's made of Emerald Crystal from Coalisland—lovely, but certainly not worth any fortune. At least...not to anyone else." Anngret Fahey's eyes were as misty as the air around them, and Robin realized at once what this was costing her.

"I think you should keep this," Robin said gently. She refolded the tissue.

"No, Robin. I don't need it any more. Don't you see?" The lady's head was held high, and she was smiling brightly through her unshed tears. "In meeting you I've come to terms with all of this. Let me tell you about the rosary." She led them to a nearby bench beneath a tree. Greg wiped it off with his handkerchief so they could sit.

"I was with Sean when he bought the rosary," she said. "It didn't matter to me that he was Catholic or from the Republic. Nothing mattered except that I loved him." She smiled briefly. "That part I know you've already guessed. I didn't tell Fiona, and I took great care not to introduce him to her because I knew the effect she'd have on him, the effect she had on all men. Oh, I had no illusions of his loving me. I was his good friend, like a cherished cousin, but I thought that perhaps in time...." She sighed. "Well, it was inevitable that he should meet Fiona. It was like something from your Hollywood cinema—one look at her fiery hair and personality to match and Sean was captured forever. He loved her enough to give up everything—his home, his family, his church. As it says in the Good Book, her people became his people, her cause became his cause."

Anngret Fahey took the rosary from Robin, entwined it in her fingers, and held it up. Even in the morning mist, it sparkled. "Though he gave up Catholicism, he did not give up this rosary. He kept it in his pocket, which infuriated Fiona. When he died, I went with Fiona to a private viewing before his body was transported to this cemetery. At the viewing, Fiona pulled this rosary out of her own pocket. 'It meant so much to him,' she said. 'I suppose he may as well keep it.' Then she tossed it into the casket, where it slid down beside his body. A few moments later, when I paid my last respects, I removed it." She lowered her hand and her head. "'Twas a selfish gesture, and I've felt guilty for it all these years. Until now. Please take it, Robin," she said, holding it out. "I *know* this is what Sean would have wanted."

Robin closed her fingers around the rosary. Then she put her arms around the lady, who was truly a lady, and wept openly. For everything.

CHAPTER 21

They arrived in Ballylith late that night and went straight to their rooms in Reilly Castle.

Next morning after breakfast Robin invited Gilda Lynch into the small sitting room for a private discussion, just the two of them.

"Is it to be a frank chat then?" Gilda asked as they were seated.

Robin sat back in her chair and cupped her cold hands around a mug of hot tea. "That's right, Gilda. We've a lot to discuss. Not only what happened in the past, but what is to happen in the future—yours, Wrenny's, and mine." She paused for a sip of tea. "I know about my parents now, about Sean Reilly and Fiona Morrison. I even saw their graves."

Gilda clasped her hands over her heart. "No! Ye didn't!"

"I did, and I'm glad. You know something, Gilda? I don't believe anyone here at Reilly Castle ever tried to understand Sean. He was a very young man, a boy really, who was in love, or at least thought he was. Maybe he was in love with an image—the glamorous, public side of Fiona Morrison; maybe she was one-dimensional; nevertheless, he loved her, and he affirmed that love by supporting her through some of the most difficult and terror-filled years of his young life. I want you to know that I admire him, Gilda. In spite of what he did, what he became, how he died, I admire him because he followed his heart. That's something not too many of us dare to do. You never knew him, did you?"

Gilda entwined her fingers in her voluminous skirt. "Ah, I knew him as a lad in the village, but I didn't come to work here at the castle until Sean was grown and gone."

"Did you know why he chose the Queen's University?" Gilda did not respond. "He wanted to see first-hand what was happening in Northern Ireland, what effect it was having on the Republic of Ireland, what it would mean to the future of his country. He *cared*. He never intended to stay there, Gilda. He had planned to come back to the Republic after a year, still Catholic. But he met Fiona. And he couldn't help himself." Gilda remained silent. "Sean died in the same battle that injured Wrenny."

A tiny sob escaped Gilda's lips. "What happened to…herself?"

"Fiona. You may say the name here now, Gilda. It's Fiona. A sniper killed her in 1972."

Robin placed her mug on the side table and rubbed her hands up and down the sleeves of her soft, green sweater. "Gilda," she began, gently, "there's something else we have to discuss. We have to talk about the castle and about Wrenny." Gilda nodded slowly.

"Fiona was a wealthy young woman," Robin continued, "but she converted all of her wealth into two trust funds, one for Wrenny—the one that provides her personal allowance—and one for me. I must go to Tralee and talk with Mr. O'Sullivan, but I want you to think about something while I'm gone. I don't need my trust fund. I'd like to use it to refurbish the castle and make it into a fine inn, something that would attract visitors to Ballylith. This is a beautiful area, the kind of quiet beauty that many people look for and never find. On the other hand, I can't stay here and take care of the castle. I have a good job in America, one that I like very much, and I want to return there to live. I could visit Ireland two or three times a year. You see, I would need someone I can trust to supervise things here.

"The other thing I want you to think about is Wrenny. I want very much to take her with me to America, but I don't want to uproot her from all that's familiar to her, from all that she loves. That's another reason for making the castle more comfortable. It's Wrenny's home. When Greg and I leave for Florida in a few days, we'd like to take her with us for a visit; then, I'll bring her back, personally, after the first of the year. Beyond that, I would arrange for her to visit me as often as she'd like. Think about these things, Gilda. When I return from Tralee, we'll talk again."

Robin stood. "This afternoon Wrenny will be going with us. I promised her a little adventure. We'll spend the night, see Mr. O'Sullivan in the morning, do something fun for Wrenny, and return tomorrow evening."

As Robin left the room, she heard Gilda's huge sigh. It sounded like a good sigh, one of relief.

~~~

Fergus Halloran arrived with the morning mail. There was a letter for Greg from his grandmother.

"Oh, Greg! What does she have to say? How did she find us? They couldn't possibly have received our postcards yet. Could they?" Robin and

Greg sat on the stone stoop in front of the castle, where the sun shone warmly through the nippy air, cleaning up all traces of morning dew.

"One question at a time," Greg answered. "This letter was forwarded by O'Sullivan. I had given Gran his address as a precaution. Hope nothing's wrong." He opened the letter, glanced through it, then began to read aloud from his grandmother's very precise, spidery handwriting:

Dear Greg,

This is a "good news" letter. Wonderful things have been happening around here, and I couldn't wait to tell you. (I do believe that letter-writing is considered good exercise for someone my age!)

First, Cassie and Jerome have a new baby girl. (Picture enclosed) Her name is Oriole Alice Davis—Alice for Cassie's mother, Strawberry Alice, and Oriole as some sort of tribute to Robin—a bird. Is that a compliment?

Robin laughed. "I love it! Wait until we get Wrenny home—there'll be three 'birds' on the plantation. Where's the picture?"

Greg reached into the envelope and pulled out a snapshot of Baby Oriole, dark and lovely against white blankets. "She's beautiful!" Robin exclaimed. "But I thought the baby wasn't due until the twelfth. Read some more!"

Oriole was nine days early and weighs only six pounds, six ounces, but she's a healthy little charmer. Cassie, Jerome, and Berry went out for Thanksgiving dinner, and that baby so close! Imagine going to a restaurant for Thanksgiving, never mind the baby! I guess times are different now. Cassie says to tell Robin hello and to please hurry home.

Greg, dear, your editor has been calling. She's not very pleased about being unable to reach you. Please give her a call.

We had a lovely time last week with a hunting party from Michigan. There were four men, and they brought their wives with them. The wives didn't hunt. They did some shopping and relaxing and "tea-partying," which was a nice change for me. I do so enjoy spending time with Northern women. I love listening to them talk! Ned and Jody took the hunters, along with the dogs, Max and Chess. They went on horseback. (The men, that is, not the dogs.)

Well, dear, I believe this is enough exercise for one day. I'll be glad to have you and Robin home. Speaking of Robin—we have a nice surprise waiting for her. Also speaking of Robin—in all this time you've been gone, have you noticed how ...

Greg suddenly quit reading. "Come on," Robin prompted. "What were you supposed to notice?"

Greg chuckled. "Gran's a mess," he said.

"Come on, let me read it!" Robin snatched the letter from his hands and read aloud:

... have you noticed how lovely and talented and well-spoken she is?

Robin nudged Greg with her elbow. "Have you noticed?"

"She hasn't heard you in a fit of temper," he replied.

"Oh, listen to this!" She read:

Have you noticed her, dear? Sometimes the best things in life are to be found not in faraway places but right on your own doorstep.
Love,
Gran

"You know what?" Greg asked.

"What?"

"Gran may have a surprise waiting for you at the plantation, but I think we have one for her, too. Don't we?"

Robin turned, her face just inches from his. "Do we?" she whispered.

He kissed her lightly on the lips. "You already know I love you. Will you marry me?"

"Oh, yes!" she cried, throwing her arms around him. "On the steps of a castle! You proposed on the steps of a castle. How romantic!"

"There's more," he said, reaching into his pocket, "something I saw in a jeweler's window while you were poking around the sweater shop in Listowel." He handed her a small box. "How would you like the romance of a Claddagh ring on your finger until we can choose a proper diamond?"

"Greg!" she squealed, extracting the exquisite silver ring from its box. A small heart was held by two hands, and a tiny crown rested atop the heart.

He slipped it onto her right hand with the heart turned inward. "This means you're 'spoken for,'" he said. "If the heart is turned outward, you're available. On the left hand it means you're married. It signifies friendship, loyalty, and love. Old Irish tradition."

Robin was overcome. "It's beautiful," she managed to say, admiring its delicate sparkle in the sunlight. She hugged him tightly one more time. "And I don't want a 'proper diamond,'" she whispered into his ear. "This means much more to me."

Just then Fergus, coughing loudly and grinning like a Cheshire, passed in front of them, pushing a wheelbarrow full of manure. "'Scuse me, folks. Got to get that pesky flower garden shaped up. Gilda says it's an eyesore."

Robin held her nose, and Greg laughed. "You were right. This is so romantic."

The Claddagh Ring

~~~

. Greg called his editor, who needed a clarification that could be handled over the phone, and Robin went to the tower room to help Wrenny pack an overnight bag.

"What fun!" Wrenny exclaimed as she stood near the wardrobe selecting an outfit. "I haven't been to Tralee since Auntie Maeve took me. A long time ago, it was."

More than twenty years, thought Robin. She, too, would be having fun—the fun of watching Wrenny's pleasure, of seeing things through her eyes, the eyes of a child. She sat on the edge of the bed. "Wrenny," she said, "when we get back from Tralee, it will be time for Greg and me to go home to America." Wrenny whipped around, dropping the skirt she held. Robin added quickly, "We'd like to take you with us for a visit; then, you could come back to Ballylith after Christmas. Would you like that?"

Wrenny's eyes widened with joy. "Ohhh, America!" She ran to Robin and flopped down beside her on the bed. "Do you mean it? Do you really mean it?"

"I certainly do. I want to show you my home and introduce you to my friends. Oh, I just thought of something," she added, reaching into her pocket. "My best friend, Cassie Davis, just had a baby girl. We'll be able to see the baby when we get there."

"Baby? I see babies sometimes in the village when Peig Morgan takes me. So soft and sweet they are. I love babies!"

"Look here. This baby's name is Oriole." Robin handed the snapshot to Wrenny.

"Oh, dear! Oh, *dear*!" Wrenny's face pinched up with grief as she looked at the photo.

"What's the matter?"

"The baby. It…it's *burned*!"

And Wrenny Reilly learned about black people.

~~~

They arrived in Tralee in time to check into the Grand Hotel on Denny Street and to locate an interesting pub, one with good food and entertainment. One Wrenny would enjoy. It was interesting to Robin that Irish pubs were family affairs. Children sat around heavy oak tables with their parents, having just as good a time as the older folks.

The pub they chose advertised "pub grub"—spicy soup, thick sandwiches, and cheese and onion crisps, all delicious. Greg ordered a mug of Guinness stout and waited patiently while the proprietor poured and scraped, poured and scraped, until the mug had exactly the right amount of liquid and the right amount of creamy white head.

Robin watched in fascination. Wrenny, on the other hand, was fascinated with a picture on the wall behind their table. It was a large color photograph of the current "Rose of Tralee," an Irish beauty newly crowned at the festival in September.

"A princess!" she said, gazing upward. "A beautiful princess, would you look at the gown now! 'Tis all sparkly!"

This was Wrenny's day for fun, and anything that pleased her also pleased Robin and Greg. She especially enjoyed the "Sham-Rock" music, played by a group of rosy-cheeked young men. It reminded Greg of rock music played and sung in America—lively and loud! When the group took their break, the publican introduced an interesting bit of musical contrast, a whistler! It seemed he could whistle just about anything and beautifully too. His tunes reminded Robin, very sweetly, of Patrick.

"Could you *please* whistle 'The Last Rose of Summer?'" Wrenny called to the whistler. He did so immediately, and she giggled with delight. In a corner, three very old women enjoyed it as much as Wrenny did, swaying back and forth, back and forth, puffing on their pipes.

"The whistler gets better as he's had himself a drop," said the waiter, refilling Greg's mug.

"Do you ever have bagpipe music in here?" Robin asked suddenly. "I heard somewhere that bagpipes originated in Ireland."

"Aye, they did that," answered the waiter. "But the pipes are mostly in Scotland now." He leaned in closer and lowered his voice. "Y' see, when we Irish introduced whiskey along with kilts and bagpipes to our neighbor, Scotland, the poor Scots didn't realize that the last two were a joke!" He straightened and walked away, roaring with laughter.

When they left the pub, they took a bus (at Wrenny's insistence) to a production of Siamsa Tire, the Folk Theatre of Ireland. It was lively, colorful, and fairly short; even so, it was past midnight when the three returned to the hotel, Greg to his room, and Robin and Wrenny to theirs.

Wrenny fell asleep immediately. Before Robin turned out the light, she leaned over to brush the hair from Wrenny's eyes and kissed her on the forehead. Wrenny smiled in her sleep...and Robin smiled, too.

~~~

Next morning at ten o'clock the three travelers arrived at O'Sullivan's office by appointment. During her first visit, Robin had not noticed the sign on his desk: *Kern O'Sullivan, Solicitor, Trusts and Estates.* Now she had a lot of questions about those very things.

"My, oh my!" the young O'Sullivan said, jumping to his feet. "So there be two of you, and the second every bit as lovely as the first!" His face was a study in fascination.

"This is Wren Reilly, Mr. O'Sullivan," Robin said. "My sister. My sister, whom I never would have had the pleasure of meeting, if you hadn't been that wee bit careless."

"Well then, Miss, if you're pleased, I'm pleased. Shall we get started?"

Much to Robin's surprise, Kern O'Sullivan took a great deal of time explaining Ronan Reilly's will and the disposition of the two trust funds left by Fiona Morrison and smartly invested by the bank's trust officer. Robin was amazed at the amount of money that would be available.

Wrenny, oblivious to the discussion, played with a wooden puzzle on a low table while O'Sullivan patiently answered all of Robin's questions and gave her copies of the will, including documents to sign for proceeding with probate.

He ended by saying, "Though I could have cleared up a wee bit o' the problems on the first day you were here, I could not have told you who Wren was, or who Fiona Morrison was, other than her name. I didn't know. And I was never told about Sean Reilly. The papers I have here, which of course, were in the care of my dear departed grandfather, identified Sean only as Tomas's son. That he was your father, I surely didn't know."

"You've been very kind, Mr. O'Sullivan. If I seemed impatient when I first met you, I apologize."

"Understandable, and I accept."

Arrangements were made for Robin's trust fund to be used for the refurbishment of Reilly Castle. Wrenny's allowance was raised appropriately, and her accommodations at "the home" were canceled. That would please Gilda Lynch.

Robin stood, drawing their meeting to a close. "Thank you for taking so much time with us."

"Ah, well," O'Sullivan replied, "when God made time, he made plenty of it!"

CHAPTER 22

They arrived home at Reilly Castle just as Gilda was laying out the evening meal.

"Plain food, it is," Gilda explained, "since we've no guests, just we four and Fergus, he's been workin' late and hungry."

"Ummm," was Wrenny's happy comment as they sat down to hot mashed potatoes mixed with onions and cabbage. Robin forced a smile. She was still a long way from a hamburger and fries.

"I've been thinkin' about what y' said yesterday, about the castle and Wrenny 'n all," said Gilda as they began the meal. "Fergus and me, we talked about it some."

"And?"

"And, well, we think it's a fine idea, to put the castle to rights, get folks comin' to Ballylith. Ye'r right about it being pretty here. It's special, the quiet, the niceness of it all. It could be a grand place...but...."

"But what, Gilda?"

"Well, y' see," Fergus injected, "Gilda and me, we wouldn't want left out 'n all."

"Left out? Why would you be left out?"

Fergus shrugged. "With you hirin' some fancy folks to run things, they mightn't want us."

Robin smiled. "And don't you two think you're fancy enough?" They stared at her. "I was hoping, Gilda, that you would be willing to manage the inside of the castle, with regular hired help, of course; and that you, Fergus, might consider coming here full time, maybe hiring a couple of gardeners and an extra handyman. Well, what do you say?"

Fergus's grin spread across his whole face. "More gardeners and a handyman? I say, let's get started!"

"And I say, thanks to the Holy Mother, and you, too, Robin!" Gilda blurted out. "Do ye really think we can do it?"

"I know you can. I've already asked Mr. O'Sullivan to hire a company that will do a good job of refurbishment. You two need to be here to keep things in line. Fergus, you could start right away to look for help. The cemetery needs a great deal of work; Wrenny's garden needs to be cleaned and replanted; we could use flowers and shrubbery at the entrances near the gates. You know the kinds of things that need doing."

"For sure an' I do. We'll finally be able to put these grounds to rights and that's a fact!"

Robin turned to Gilda. "Tomorrow morning, right after breakfast, I'd like you to give me a tour of the castle. I haven't seen all of it yet. Maybe we could decide if some things need to be brought out of storage; we could talk about special pieces that need to be saved and things to be discarded or sold. Tomorrow will be a full day; we'll have to do all of our packing for the trip, too, because our plane leaves Shannon at seven o'clock Friday morning. That means we need to be out of here by five-thirty."

"Ye'll be getting up mighty early, ye will," said Fergus.

Greg smiled. "True, Fergus. And I'm not worth much at that hour; however, my grandmother is expecting us for lunch." He turned to Robin. "I called her yesterday and told her to expect one more, that you had found a sister."

"I'm going to America!" Wrenny piped up suddenly. "Robin saw my room up in the tower, and now I'm going to America to see her room. But I'll come back, Gilda," she added quickly. "Robin says I can visit America often. I love Robin! And I love you, Gilda! I love *everybody*!" She jumped up and twirled.

Tears of joy dropped off Gilda's puffy cheeks, making wet splashes on her napkin. "I love you, too, dear. And I'll be thankin' the Holy Mother again and again for sending Robin to us when She did."

Fergus pulled Greg aside as they left the kitchen. With his leprechaun grin and bright eyes shining, he spoke softly, "About our Robin...I saw the Claddagh ring on her finger. And I'm thinkin' ye might have nicer legs than yer own under yer table before the new spuds are up!"

Greg laughed aloud.

~~~

"I'm taking Liam O'Byrne his pint," Greg said next morning as Robin and Gilda began their walk through the castle. "Wrenny's going with me."

"Liam!" Gilda said. "Now there's a one! Don't see him a'tall anymore, he's so old and in that wheelchair, but Bridget says he's cranky as ever. Gives her a bit o' trouble betimes, swears a bunch, but Liam's a good man. Now how do you expect to get a pint past Bridget? Speaks straight to the Holy Ghost, she does."

Greg winked. "I'll think of something." He gave Robin a quick kiss and left with Wrenny.

Robin had already seen most of the downstairs, but there was a small library, which she hadn't seen, next to Wrenny's music room. It was dark and dusty from lack of use, and it smelled of old paper. Robin thought it would make a nice reading room for guests if it had good lighting and comfortable furniture. And some new books.

"Now, if this were a big castle," Gilda said, "there'd be a wee chapel off the Hall. As it is, we use the Hall for prayers, like the family did all those years past. There's a small wine cellar, but I don't think ye'll be wantin' to go down there. As far as I know, it hasn't been looked into since Mr. Reilly was a young man. We'd have to take a lantern, for the steps are all crumbly, and there's no electricity down there. 'Twas a dungeon when the castle was built. Gives me the jitters, it does."

"We'll pass on the dungeon. Let's go to the top and work down."

They went up three flights of stairs to the cold, damp and clammy attic.

"Reilly Castle has a ghost, y' know," Gilda said, not looking particularly worried.

"A nice one, I hope."

"No, he's a bad one, he is. Came here as a guard when the castle was first built, but then one night when he'd had himself a drop too many, he scaled the walls and climbed in the window where the young Miss was sleeping. Tried to have his way with her, he did, but the plucky lass fought him off, biting and kicking, and finally pushed him out the window. Died as soon as he hit the ground, and good riddance, too. Now he walks these halls at night, groaning and clanking as ghosts do." Gilda paused for effect, glancing at Robin. "Have ye been hearing him then?"

Robin laughed. "No, but it's a good story. I'll bet our paying guests would enjoy it."

Gilda's face relaxed into a grin. "They do," she said. "It's part o' me spiel."

~~

In the attic they found some fine pieces of Chippendale furniture on its way to ruin. There were other treasures—a gilt mirror, some Waterford crystal, some badly tarnished silver. Also tons of rotted clothing. Gilda noted things that would need immediate rescue.

On the next floor down, the four large bedrooms were closed but still furnished, except for a missing painting or, Gilda said, a lamp here and there, which she had sold.

"What is this?" Robin asked, rubbing her hand across the rough wall surface in one especially charming room.

"Those are old cut-out prints that a lady o' the house pasted directly on the walls. 'Twas a fad of much earlier times."

The last floor to view was the bedroom floor currently in use. These rooms were much smaller, cozier, than those on the floor above. In addition to Robin's and Greg's rooms, there was one other open to guests—the tower room opposite Wrenny's. It was clean and furnished nicely, though not elegantly. Nearby was Gilda's room, stuffed full of personal belongings accumulated over thirty-three years. It was as neat as possible under the circumstances but definitely overwhelming.

"One favor I'd like to ask ye," Gilda said as they stood inside her doorway.

"What is it?"

"I'd really like to be moving into me own wee house across the road. I told you Mr. Reilly had it fixed up ever so nice for me, for when Wrenny left, that is. Do ye think I could live there and still take care o' Wrenny and the castle? We'll have a live-in girl, o' course—Peig Morgan's daughter's been wantin' work. She can keep Wrenny company at night."

"I think that's a fine idea, Gilda. Why don't you plan to move as soon as we leave? Wrenny will be out of your way for a month or so, and you'll have some time before the refurbishment gets started. Fergus can help you."

"Oh, bless you, dear! Sure 'n I'd like to spread out me things more than I can in this wee room. Come, let me show you Mr. Reilly's room." She led the way to one of the three closed rooms at the other end of the hall.

It was typical male paradise—dark colors and leather, an inlaid writing table. Nothing that would give a clue to Ronan's personality, other than the "blathering television," to which Fergus had referred more than once.

"He played the television early in the morning and late at night, he did. In his last months, though, he left it on all the time. It was loud, too, since himself was hard o' hearing. Fergus used to complain something awful in the mornings when Mr. Reilly had his windows open. 'Course he did all his complaining to me, much good that did!"

Across the hall was Maeve Reilly's room. "It's just as she left it," Gilda said, opening the door. "Mr. Reilly wouldn't hear of changing a thing."

It was a pretty room, decorated in lavender and white. The furniture was old and elegant; the posts on the bed reached nearly to the ceiling. The problem was…magazines. Piles of them!

"I told you she was a one for her magazines," Gilda said. They were everywhere! Piled on tables, on chairs, on the floor, some of them nearly forty years old, Robin saw at a glance.

"Did she really read them all?"

"Read them at night, she did. And look here." Gilda stooped down and pulled a dress box from under the bed, putting it atop the quilt. It was full of yellowed clippings—household articles and recipes. "Sometimes she'd bring me a clipping or two," Gilda recalled, fondly, "and we'd talk about it, about how certain curtains might look in the kitchen, or how a fancy new chair would look in the drawing room. Never did anything about it, o' course. There wasn't the money. But we tried some recipes, we did. Some mighty funny ones," she added with a quick laugh. Then she sighed. "I need to be getting these magazines out o' here, don't I?"

"I'm afraid so, Gilda. If nothing else, they're a fire hazard." She looked around. "This room would be a good place to begin. You'll have a lot of cleaning and sorting to do all over the castle before the work crew can start. I hope you'll be able to locate some good help."

"Oh my, yes I will. Besides Peig Morgan's daughter, there's Rose O'Hanlon with a good strong back. She'd like a job, I know she would."

"Well, I'll leave it to you."

As they started out, Robin bumped into a stack of magazines near the wardrobe, and the stack fell over. Beneath it was another dress box. She pulled it out and removed the cover, expecting to find more household clippings and recipes. There were no recipes, but the nature of the clippings inside the box caused her to sit on the floor, stunned. All of them concerned the troubles in Northern Ireland, and many of them referred to Fiona Morrison; some even had pictures of her. Robin held one up, as Gilda squatted beside her on the floor.

"My goodness, gracious!" Gilda exclaimed. "Is that herself now? I never knew what she looked like."

"It's herself all right—my mother, Fiona."

"She's...well, she's very beautiful."

That certainly was an understatement. Fiona Morrison was the most exquisite creature Robin had ever seen. She was standing on a hill, speaking to a gathering of folk who were seated on the grass. Her arms were raised; the wind was blowing her thin dress and thick mane of shining red hair. In a close-up shot, her deep-set eyes proved to be as green as the grass on which her audience was seated. She was full of life and youth and excitement and purpose. Who could blame Sean Reilly for falling in love with her?

Robin carefully lifted out more clippings and found some that referred to Sean. Those passages had been lovingly underlined.

"Do ye suppose this is why she subscribed to all those magazines? To get word of young Sean?"

"I think so, Gilda," Robin replied slowly. "How else could she learn anything of him? Ronan had disowned him and didn't want his name spoken."

"Well, now, Mr. Reilly would have sworn up a mighty cloud o' steam if he'd known about this!"

"I suspect that's why this box was hidden. I'm wondering, too, Gilda, if Mr. Reilly's preoccupation with television wasn't for the same purpose—to get word of Sean."

Gilda was awestruck. "Ye think so?"

Robin nodded. "I do. You said he turned it on early in the morning and late at night—those are two important times for news reports."

"Oh, my! Why couldn't those nice folks—and they *were* nice, Robin— why couldn't they have talked about Sean together instead of sneaking around so?"

"Stubbornness. Mr. O'Sullivan said that Ronan was not a mean man. I believe he was just plain stubborn. He probably thought that if he held out long enough, Sean would see the error of his ways and come home." Tears began to form. "But he didn't consider Fiona. My guess is that he and Maeve didn't even know about Wrenny and me until Fiona sent us here. What a waste of years and love."

"Well, now," Gilda began cautiously, "are ye sure y' want to see the last bedroom? The one that belonged to ye'r daddy?"

"My...my daddy? Oh, yes," Robin replied. "Most certainly, yes!" She wiped her eyes with the back of her hand and stood, clutching the magazine with Fiona's pictures close to her chest.

As Gilda unlocked the door to Sean's room, she said, "Other than meself now and then, to dust up a bit, no one's been in here for years. Mrs. Reilly used to come some when Mr. Reilly was away. She'd just walk around and look, touch a few things and leave." She stepped aside to let Robin enter.

My father's room, Robin thought, with more than a few butterflies in her stomach. It was like taking a giant step backward in time. The walls were decorated with posters from the late nineteen-fifties and early sixties. School memorabilia was scattered haphazardly, and a now-antiquated record player rested on top of a footlocker. She walked slowly around the room, delighted to find it packed with personality.

"Most of his things are still here," Gilda said. "After I came to live here, I did give his clothes to the poor as Mrs. Reilly instructed, and, of course, Sean took a fair amount o' odds 'n ends with him when he left."

There were some sports trophies on the mantle, including a junior trophy for marksmanship. A side table held two car models, which Sean had obviously labored over as a child; the paint was streaked and the glue was thick and smeary.

"I also got rid of old school books and class papers, and some stacks of car magazines. Mr. Reilly said, 'Clean it all out,' but Mrs. Reilly had such a look on her face as told me not to clean too much, if y' know what I mean. The drawers are all empty and the wardrobe, too." Gilda moved to the bed and lovingly ran her hands across the covering. "This old quilt was his favorite. Had it from the time he was a nipper, he did."

Robin swallowed hard. Despite the chill in the cold room, she felt warm inside. Strangely, this was the first time since coming to Reilly Castle that she had considered the building anything more than a musty old monument. This room, at least, had been a home. And suddenly, in this moment, Robin felt the first stirrings of true kinship with its owner. She pulled out the chair in front of the small desk and sat down, a little weak-kneed.

"That picture is Sean; seventeen, he was," Gilda said.

Robin lifted the framed photo off the desk and held it lovingly in both hands. He was a handsome boy with a winning smile, dressed for hunting, holding a rifle, standing at the edge of a woods. A hunter. Her father. And she looked like him.

Gilda's voice again. "That book I couldn't bear to burn, nor could I look at it, so private an' all. But it seems to me you should see it, if ye be wanting to."

Robin picked up the book, the only other item on the desk. It was a journal with no more than twenty or so entries, progressing from the first in a childlike scrawl, to the last in a student's meticulous handwriting. Feeling like an intruder, yet too curious to stop herself, Robin read a few pages then turned to the final entry:

I saw a parched desert
And dreamed I crossed it.
I saw a wide river
And dreamed I swam it.
I saw a tall mountain
And dreamed I climbed it.
I saw a fierce problem
And dreamed I solved it.

He had dreamed it. Maybe he could have done it all, if it hadn't been for Fiona, for the blinding light she had been.

Robin sat quietly for a few moments then rose slowly, picking up the photograph and the journal. She would take them and the magazine with Fiona's pictures with her. Tangible reminders of her elusive heritage. Reminders of who and what she was. And still could be.

~~~

The plane departed Shannon at 7:02 a.m. on Friday, and no one on the aircraft could possibly have been more excited than Wrenny Reilly. Her hair was caught up in a clip from which curls cascaded in wild abandon, matching her mood. Pretty as a spring day, she was. Strapped into her window seat next to Robin, she closed her eyes then opened them wide, then looked out the window, then closed her eyes again, the same routine over and over, punctuated with squeals of delight and sudden gales of laughter. She squeezed Robin's hand tightly, and Greg, on the other side of Robin, squeezed her other hand. Robin felt very much at peace, the happiest and most content she'd been in many weeks.

Changing planes in Atlanta proved to be as much an adventure for Wrenny as the long flight had been. Shuttle trains, escalators, vendors, and mechanical voices over a public address system—all were new to the child who had never been farther than Limerick and Tralee.

"Wrenny, you mustn't stare at people," Robin said. "It isn't polite." She pulled her sister along as they made their way through the terminal building.

"But he's...she's...they're...*black,* like the baby."

"You'll see more black people when we get home."

Wrenny's attention was immediately diverted to a concession, where a child was chomping on a foot-long hotdog. "Oohh! What's that?"

Greg took her hand. "Come on. I'll buy you one."

Wrenny thoroughly enjoyed her first jumbo hot dog smothered with mustard and onions. And Robin had the hamburger she'd been craving!

Robin learned, too, very quickly, that watching Wrenny in such a busy, public place took as much energy and careful attention as watching a child. Wrenny was too outgoing, too friendly, too trusting. It would be easy for an unscrupulous person to take advantage of her. Especially a predator who would recognize that she was an adult and realize within minutes that she was childlike, malleable. Wrenny was physically beautiful, and her innocence gave her an unusual, ethereal quality. If she stayed in America, even for short visits, she would have to be taught things that she had never needed to know in Ballylith.

PART III

MONTICELLO, FLORIDA
HOMECOMING

CHAPTER 23

When Greg pulled up in front of the Big House, Mrs. Haviland and Berry Wheeler were waiting on the front porch between the huge white columns. The gatekeeper had informed them that Greg was home.

Though they had left Ireland in the morning and arrived home at lunchtime, it actually had been close to twelve hours' traveling time. Wrenny and Robin were both sound asleep.

Greg hurried up the steps to give his grandmother a kiss and a hug.

"I've missed you, dear," said Mrs. Haviland, and Berry added, "The place jes ain't the same with you gone, Mr. Greg."

"We've had quite an adventure," he replied. "Come, I want you both to see what's in the car." He led them down the steps to the circular driveway.

"Land sakes! They's two Robins!" Berry exclaimed, peering in the side windows. Robin's head was leaning against the passenger door, and Wrenny was curled up in the back seat.

"Twins? Greg, you didn't say Wrenny was her *twin*." A big smile came over Mrs. Haviland's wrinkled face. "They are absolutely lovely together!"

"Gran," Greg said, weighing his next words carefully, "Wrenny is…well, she's not exactly retarded—she's very bright—but her mind isn't at the same level as her age. It never will be. In Ireland she's called an 'innocent,' and the term suits her very well."

Just then Robin stirred in the front seat. She rubbed her eyes and looked up then quickly opened the door and got out. "Greg! Why didn't you wake me? I didn't have a chance to brush my hair!" She hugged Mrs. Haviland, then Berry, saying, "Is it morning? If it is, then good morning to you both. It's so good to be home! And I want you to meet my sister. Wrenny! Wrenny, dear, wake up. We're home!"

She opened the back door, and Wrenny, who woke very quickly, hopped out, all smiles. But when she saw Berry, her eyes widened and her mouth popped open in awe.

Robin explained, "Berry, other than those who walked quickly past us at the Atlanta airport, you're the first black person Wrenny has ever seen. Up close. Say something, so she'll know you're real."

Berry grinned, showing her beautiful white teeth. "Welcome home, chile. We sho is glad you heah!"

Wrenny clapped her hands over her mouth and giggled.

~~~

Berry served lunch in the small dining room. When they had finished eating, Mrs. Haviland, Greg and Robin took their tall glasses of iced tea to the enclosed sun porch while Wrenny wandered through the plantation house with Berry, touching and stroking every object within reach.

With Greg's encouragement, Robin told Mrs. Haviland about the trip to Ireland, about Ronan and Maeve Reilly, Belfast and Londonderry, Sean and Fiona, about Wrenny's injury, and about the refurbishment of Reilly Castle. The telling was catharsis. All of her emotions, bottled up like Gilda's fruit, came pouring out through her words.

"Wrenny's going to stay with me until after Christmas," Robin finished, "then I'll take her back to Ballylith. Miss Emily, I know you'll need the garage home for Patrick's replacement, so I'll be moving to my Tallahassee apartment as soon as I can get packed."

"Well, dear," the lady said, "the plantation is your home. You grew up here. It's not as if you just stopped by for a month or two." She lifted the tea pitcher with practiced grace and began refilling the glasses. "I wrote you about a little surprise, and this is it: the overseer's cottage on the northeast end, near the Ashville Road gate, has been empty now for two years. You know that John Crockett prefers to live closer to the other side of the plantation, nearer his workers. Well, I've had the cottage cleaned and redecorated, and I want you to live in it, rent-free of course. Let's say you'll be house-sitting for me. I really do need someone in that cottage to keep it from deteriorating."

"Miss Emily, I'm overwhelmed! That's a very generous offer." Robin was well aware that the "cottage" was a finely appointed two-story brick home with a beautiful yard and privacy fence.

"And we accept your offer with pleasure," said Greg, quickly.

"We?" The older woman was speechless, holding her breath. Dare she hope?

"You're not the only one with a surprise, Gran. Robin has agreed to marry me."

Mrs. Haviland let out her breath in a long, happy sigh. "Oh, my dears!"

"Would this...be acceptable to you, Miss Emily?" Robin asked, softly and politely, thinking of her own humble beginnings.

Mrs. Haviland clasped her hands to her heart. "It's what I've been *praying* for! Oh, dear, I shouldn't have said that." She blushed. "Such bad manners."

"Thanks, Gran," said Greg. "I know you love her. Almost as much as I do." The look he then gave Robin dispelled all her lingering doubts. A warm sensation ignited in the core of her body and spread throughout, and she felt as if she would melt into a wonderful, sticky puddle!

~~~

Later, Robin, Wrenny, and Greg visited Cassie and Jerome Davis and their new baby. Oriole, sweet and charming, was zipped into a fuzzy sleeper, and she won Wrenny's heart immediately.

"Oh, she's beautiful!" Wrenny said, stroking the baby's arm, looking from her to the parents and back again. She was still awed by their color. "Will Oriole grow up talking funny then, like Robin and Greg?"

Jerome laughed. "Prob'ly worse," he drawled.

"Could I *please* help take care of her? I'm good with babies, I am. Many's the time I helped Peig Morgan with Marin, her wee granddaughter. I sang to her and played my harp." She looked at Cassie. "Do you have a harp?"

"A h-harp?" Cassie was enchanted with this lovely girl. "No," she said, "I'm afraid we don't have a harp."

"No matter. I can sing without one. Robin taught me a new song—'Follow the fellow who follows a dream!'" Taken with the alliteration, Wrenny repeated it to the baby, "Follow the fellow who follows a dream; follow the fellow who follows a dream, follows a dream, follows a dream. "

The Robin...the Wren...and the Oriole.

CHAPTER 24

Late that night, Greg and Robin sat on the glider on Robin's front porch, which overlooked the long oval driveway. Beneath them on both ends of the pillared garage, old-fashioned carriage lanterns (modernized with electricity) lit the parking area and cast a faint yellow glow upward—a sort of artificial moonlight on a moonless night.

"I didn't ask whether you wanted the cottage," Greg said. "I should have."

"I thought that was obvious. It's a beautiful place! Who wouldn't want it?"

"But we haven't had time to talk about…well, anything. Where we'll live, how we'll live. Things have happened fast. Surprised the hell out of me, frankly."

Robin smiled. "Me, too. I worried that your grandmother wouldn't want me. As a family member, I mean."

"Are you serious?"

"Very. My father—Patrick, that is—was your hired help. Hardly in the same class as a Haviland."

"If you know my grandmother as well as I think you do, you know that she doesn't think in terms of class. She never has. Tradition, values, propriety— yes. But never class distinction. That's for the ladies who belong to clubs and talk about their money and possessions and wonder why they're not invited to Gran's little tea parties. When I fell in love with you, I never considered anything but the person of Robin Reilly. I wasn't interested in your ancestry. Only in you." He squeezed her hand, and she leaned her head over on his shoulder.

"But you helped me discover who I am."

"No. We discovered where you came from. That's different. The trekking and tracing all over Ireland was interesting to me, but only because it was important to you. I love you." He lifted her chin with his hand and kissed her lovingly and deeply. "And now," he said, gently releasing her, "what shall we do about the cottage?"

"Live in it, of course."

"Do you mean that?"

"Well, the plantation is home for both of us." She lifted her shoulders in a grand shrug and said with an Irish lilt, "I'm thinking there's no place I'd rather be and that's a fact."

He kissed her again, this time his hands moving tenderly over the swell of her firm breasts. "Wait," she whispered.

"Why?" he whispered back.

"We're not done talking."

"We've got a lifetime to talk."

Gently, she pushed him away. "What about your job and mine?"

"What about them?"

"You travel a lot, and I work in Tallahassee."

"I know that." He tried nibbling at her ear.

"Greg! What I mean is, will you expect me to quit my job?"

"Only if you want to."

"I don't. It means a great deal to me."

"Will you expect me to quit *my* job?"

"Don't be silly."

"You realize that I won't be home every night watching the 'blathering television.'"

Robin laughed. "And I thank the Blessed Mother for that! Oh, there's one more thing." Her smiled was suddenly gone. "I can't quit hunting, Greg. It's in my blood. I love the woods, the guns, the dogs, the quarry. Those things are important to me."

"I can live with that, provided you'll take me with you once in a while and let me shoot with my camera. Leaving your gun at home, of course," he added.

Robin threw her arms around him and hugged him tightly. Even now, she was astonished that he returned her love. She felt that she didn't deserve him. He, on the other hand, was frightened of her in a wild, exciting way. It wasn't the comfortable kind of love he had always expected to find. He almost worshiped her.

Slowly, they slid sideways, until they were lying down on the glider. Greg began unbuttoning Robin's blouse. "Are we through talking?" he whispered.

"Ummhmm," she replied, reaching for him…touching him in a way that left no room for doubt.

It was a warm December for Florida, but without clothes, on an open-air screened porch, it was downright chilly. They never noticed. And the glider swayed back and forth...back and forth....

~~~

The early morning mist was heavy at Oakfield Cemetery—a "soft day," reminiscent of Ireland—as Robin stood alone at the foot of Patrick's and Anna's graves, Sean's rosary entwined in her fingers. No sun peeked over the horizon to take away the chill. No birds sang. The only bit of brightness was the bouquet of winter roses Robin had placed between the headstones of...her parents. She knew that now. Sean and Fiona had given her life, but Patrick and Anna had given her love.

Remember the old Irish proverb, Patrick? she asked, silently. *I'm thinking of the one that says, "Sometimes you must go far to find what is near." Well, I've done just that. I've been on a long journey. Not just a physical journey, across the ocean, but an emotional journey as well. I don't pretend to understand completely your reasons for not telling me about my past, but dear Patrick, I've enough o' the Irish in me to understand a wee bit o' the way you think. I know that your motives were pure and good, and that you believed in what you did. Or didn't do. I know you loved me as your very own daughter. No one could have had a better father.*

She looked at the other headstone. *And, Anna, I'm sorry we didn't have more time together, and I'm sorry I didn't learn anything about you in Ireland. Perhaps one day I will. But thank you, Anna, for trying to keep Wrenny and me together.* Tears suddenly filled Robin's eyes. "I'm so glad to have her with me now," she whispered.

Fiercely, she wiped at the tears and turned back to Patrick. She could see him clearly, leaning against his own headstone, his chin tilted upward, a grin on his face, and a twinkle in his eye. That's the way she wanted to remember him. The way he was.

Guess what, Patrick? You're not the only one who followed a dream. Sean followed one to a sorry ending, and I'm following one, too. But I'm going to have a better time of it than Sean did. I'm going to be methodical, careful, persistent. I'm going to be like you.

Patrick's grin spread into a full smile.

But everyone's dreams are not the same, Patrick—not yours, nor Sean's, nor Ronan's, nor Greg's nor mine—and sometimes we find our dreams, even our lives, at cross-purposes. Love is the best kind of glue. I love you, Patrick. I figured out something, going through all of this, something I hadn't thought about before. And that is, we not only have to believe in the future, we also have to know what we expect of it. You'll be glad to know I expect a lot. From myself, of course. I have many dreams now, attainable dreams, and one by one, with the help of Greg and the Blessed Mother, I'll make them come true!

The mist began to lift, and shining through the wet fronds of a small cabbage palm were the first rays of sunlight. Robin pocketed the rosary and straightened her shoulders. "Patrick," she said aloud. "May you be rewarded handsomely in heaven for your goodness on this earth. And, Patrick, when it's time for that reward, 'tis no plain priest you'll have to present it but a bishop at the very least!"

Robin turned to leave. Ahead of her a rainbow arched its colors across the cemetery. Behind her, a bird sang. Or was it Patrick whistling?

Patrick's Resting Place